THE
TIME
TRINITY

Book Four of the Timepiece Series

KEVIN D. MILLER

WEBMILLER PUBLISHING

THE
TIME
TRINITY

Book Four of the Timepiece Series

By Kevin D. Miller

ISBN: 979-8-218-72020-9

For more information about the author, or to order autographed copies, visit AuthorKevinMiller.com.

PRINTED IN THE UNITED STATES OF AMERICA

DEDICATION

To Annette, my beautiful wife and life partner, and my children and grandchildren. You are the inspiration for every story in my life.

ACKNOWLEDGEMENTS

Thank you to my wife, Annette, for her contributions as my critique partner. A huge thanks to Katherine Kindred for her insights and advice.

Enjoy Other Award-Winning Books by Kevin D. Miller

THE TEMPUS GLASS
Book Three of the Timepiece Series

THE TIMEPIECE PARADOX
Book Two of the Timepiece Series

THE TIMEPIECE LEGACY
Book One of the Timepiece Series

TAQUOMA

EYES OF MORPHEUS

WHITE SKIES BLACK MINGO

HEART OF STEEL
Based on a True Story

Visit: AuthorKevinMiller.com

Please share this book with friends and family.

ONE

December 12, 1942, Honolulu, Hawaii

A cool, salty breeze inflated the bay window curtains like sleepy white sails, oblivious to the gathering storm. Squawks of gulls reminded him of home in Stinson Beach nearly a century into the future. Early morning tremors have his nerves on edge.

Bodhi sighed and sprawled in the center of the living room floor of Cassie and William's Hawaiian beach house, gripping Little William by the armpits and allowing his chubby little legs to push off the plush rug like a Russian ballet dancer. He sipped the moment like warm cocoa, the hours slipping away.

"Great leg work, Billy Boy. Ya need sturdy legs to launch a deep post or scramble for a first down, buddy." Little William cooed from his grandpa's adoring attention, blowing bubbles into words and sentences only he understood.

Elena plopped on a comfy wicker sofa next to him and tossed her floppy white hat onto a padded green chair—her thick chestnut locks in disarray after spending hours in the garden this morning.

"Ay, Papa. Don't you think he needs to grow up before you put him through your little football boot camp?"

"Ya gotta start 'em young, babe." He wrinkled his brow and cocked his head. "Whoa … What happened to your hair?"

Her nostrils flared as her eyes narrowed. "What?" She flipped her hair and glared at him. "What's wrong with my hair?"

"Um … Nothing. Nothing at all. I like what you did there."

Bodhi set the baby on the rug and bounced a small rubber ball towards him. "Fumble! Jump on it, buddy."

Elena rested her elbows on her dirt-stained knees, supporting her chin with her palms—her brows formed a creased peak as she exhaled a deep, uninspired sigh.

"What game are you listening to?"

"UCLA and Southern Cal."

"What's the score?"

"It doesn't matter. UCLA wins fourteen to seven."

"Then why listen?"

"The sheer satisfaction, sweetheart. History."

"Ajá. Sure." She rolled her eyes and ran her fingers through her tangled locks.

Bodhi lifted Little William into the air and blew raspberries on his tummy. A whiff of something foul contorted his face as if he had chomped into a mouthful of green cranberries.

"Whoa! You're a ripe little dude."

He held him with outstretched arms towards Elena and scowled.

"Take him, babe. Please."

She rose and snickered. "No way, Jose. I don't think so," she warbled in a melodic voice. "I believe a good mentor needs to learn how to change a diaper. Besides, I need to keep an eye on my carne." She pointed at the baby and winked. "Good luck with that, Coach."

Bodhi grimaced. "Wait, I need to head to Rita's to pick up Cassie and William." He shrugged and forced an exaggerated smile. "Man, I hope they, uh … had a nice honeymoon *staycation*. Where're my keys?"

Elena clicked her tongue and wagged a scolding finger. "Uh-ah. Nice try, hombre. You're not supposed to pick them up for another three hours, and I'm sure they'll be ready for some of my famous green chili by then. Don't you think?" She waved her oven mitt like a hand puppet in front of an overzealous smirk.

Little William shrieked and flailed like a flipped turtle in a fishbowl.

Bodhi pursed his lips and grunted. "Okay, okay … I hear ya, little buddy."

Elena wiped her hands on her apron as the corners of her mouth curled into a cantankerous grin. "How do you say it in football language? Oh, yeah. *Time out for equipment malfunction.*"

Bodhi glanced at Elena and winked as he passed the mashed potatoes to Cassie.

"How was the honeymoon? You kids have a good time?"

Cassie beamed and rested her hand on William's shoulder.

"It was so much fun, you guys. Rita's place is simply the best," she replied, exaggerating a pleasant sigh.

Elena filled a tumbler with iced tea as an envious expression settled across her face. Her eyebrows arched, her lips puckered, and she rested her palm on her heart.

"Aw, I want another honeymoon." She gripped Bodhi's wrist. "Take me away, Mi Amore," she pouted.

"Oh, you should do it, Elena," Cassie replied as she caught Bodhi's glare. "Dad, you guys need a break. Seriously. William and I returned so relaxed." She patted William's hand. "Right, Cappie?"

William raised an eyebrow and chuckled. "Well, some of us are relaxed. Others of us got little sleep." Cassie frowned and smacked his arm.

"Not a whole lot of places we can go, with the war on, Blondie. Hitler and the Japanese Empire put the kibosh on vacation options."

A quake sent tumblers and silverware dancing across the dining table. Lampshades fluttered, lightbulbs sizzled and dimmed. The table lurched as the floor rumbled like a five o'clock train over a cheap apartment. Fine china and crystal goblets crashed inside the curio behind them. A screech pierced the moist air like the graze of a diamond against smooth glass, shuddering the windows nearly out of their frames. The snap of electricity crackled, then fizzled, leaving a pungent odor of ozone lingering over their meal. Bodhi and Elena's eyes connected. She was thinking the same thing as him. *Government agents. Phillip. Maybe they're already on the island.*

Cassie shrilled. "What the heck was that? An earthquake? Daddy, what *was* that?"

Bodhi steadied his glass of lemonade and planted it firmly on the tabletop, jangling the ice cubes.

He glanced at Elena, then gazed at Cassie. "Blondie, there's something you should know."

"Dad! Are you joking right now? What? *What* should I know?" She gazed at him with the urgency of a person about to plunge ten stories from a burning building.

He nodded and calmly laid his palms on the table, inhaling a deep, ragged sigh. "Do you recall the agents who crashed our beach house and showed us the video of the guy who disappeared into a wormhole?"

Cassie and William glanced at each other and squeezed hands.

"Yeah. Why?" a hint of hesitation in her voice.

"I never told you who that man was."

"Seriously?" she snapped. "You knew who he was and said nothing?" Cassie shrugged, sucking nervous breaths. "Okay, so, who is he? ... Dad! Who is he?"

"A man named Phillip McMullin. Your grandfather ... my father." He grimaced, as if she were about to throw a dinner roll at him.

Cassie gasped and clamped a quivering hand over her mouth.

"How is that possible? I thought your parents died in a car accident when you were a little boy."

Bodhi shook his head and lowered his eyes. "Gram didn't exactly tell the truth about my parents, Cass."

Cassie gnawed on her clenched fist. "Dad? You're scaring me."

William placed his hand on hers and locked eyes with Bodhi.

"Is my family in danger?"

"We're *all* in danger, Will. The government possesses a third relic—the Mariner's Compass. We don't know the extent of Phillip McMullin's involvement with the relic after he escaped into the wormhole. It seems he left it in the hands of the feds when he jumped."

Cassie's expression turned troubled, and her eyes moistened. "Why would Grammy lie to you about your parents, Dad?"

Elena rested her hand on Bodhi's forearm. "Cassie, your grandparents mistreated your papa when he was only a niño. Grams protected him by sending his parents away with the timepiece. I don't think Gram meant to do it, but your grandparents were separated in time, Mija."

Cassie's eyes widened. "Oh, my God."

Elena continued, "Phillip McMullin was the man I saw years ago when we all had breakfast together on Stinson beach ... the day you dropped me off at the café to reunite with your papa."

"Are you freak'n kidding me?" She panted. "Do they know how to find us?"

Bodhi interrupted. "Phillip stole the timepiece and the Tempus Glass from us and attempted to use the combined power of all three relics to manipulate time for some unknown reason. Fortunately for us, he didn't know what the hell he was doing and failed miserably. We stole them back, Cass ... all but the compass. That's when the soldiers showed up."

"Soldiers?" she shouted. "Ah, this just keeps getting better."

"Calm down, Blondie. We escaped ... Phillip didn't."

William folded his hands, glancing at Cassie, then focusing his stare on Bodhi. "What's the plan, Bodhi? What do you need us to do?"

"I'm going to leave the timepiece with you, Blondie ... to keep safe and out of sight. Elena and I plan to return home using the hourglass."

Cassie's head snapped backward, and her eyes fluttered wildly. "What? Have you two lost your fricking minds? They'll be looking for you there."

"Cass, we're going to steal the compass. Once we have it, we'll come back for you," Bodhi replied in his calmest dad voice.

"Um ... okay. So, what does that mean, exactly? What are you going to do when you have all three relics? Take over the world?"

Bodhi hesitated and then stared deep into Cassie's eyes. "Destroy them, sweetheart."

Cassie rose and cupped her hand over her left ear. "I think I hear the baby. Hold that thought ... wait till I get back."

Bodhi glanced at Elena. The muscles in his jaws rippled. "We need to go. We've been here too long already."

Elena nodded and rested her hand over his. "We should leave now. I don't want to bring evil into this beautiful casita." She made the sign of the Cross and whispered a prayer, absently clutching a set of rosary beads.

Cassie returned with Little William saddled on her hip. She rolled her shoulders, adjusted the baby, and scoffed. "Wait. Are you guys leaving?" Her voice rose two octaves. "You're leaving right *now*?"

"We have to, Cass." He handed her Gram's music box, containing the timepiece. "Put this in a safe place and keep the timepiece well-hidden inside the box. I'm starting to believe Gram placed it inside that box on purpose ... to keep the echoes from being traced."

Bodhi bear hugged Cassie and kissed the baby on his crown. William winced as Bodhi crushed his hand. "Take care of my daughter, Will. And my grandson."

William nodded. "Yes, sir. Godspeed."

Elena lifted the baby from Cassie's arms and kissed his pink cheeks before handing him back to her.

"Stay vigilant, Mija. Pay attention to everything and everyone around you. If trouble comes, use the timepiece. Gather your familia and run like the wind."

"But ... Where would we go? I-I mean, if something happens, what do we do?"

"Trust your instincts. Disappear. Use the timepiece to go somewhere familiar and safe. Ve con Dios, Mija."

Cassie's eyes darted from Bodhi to Elena and back to Bodhi. "Can't you guys at least stay the night and leave in the morning? You haven't even tried the German chocolate cupcakes I baked for you. They're your fave, Dad."

Bodhi stuffed a cupcake in his mouth and shook his head. "Mm. We can't, Blondie. I love you, sweetheart," he said in a muffled voice. "We'll see you soon. I promise," he assured her as he wiped a spot of icing from his chin and snatched another cupcake from the tray.

TWO

April 7, 2038, Stinson Beach, California

Bodhi and Elena stepped through the portal into the darkened living room of Gram's beach house in Stinson Beach. Silence buzzed inside his ears like the chirps of cicadas in July. Eastern sunlight bathed the walls with a warm, amber glow while the rhythm of waves crashing against the shoreline and the random shrills of gulls eased the knots in his gut. They'd made it … home.

"Welcome back, Bodhi."

The gravelly voice pierced the quiet like jagged glass, firing a hot jolt of electricity up his spine. Elena clung to his elbow, scanning the dim room for the source.

Bodhi rolled his shoulders in an aggressive posture. "Phillip? What the hell? How'd you—"

"How'd I survive and escape custody? It wasn't easy, son."

"How'd you know where to find us?" Bodhi snapped.

"The night I *borrowed* your relics, I observed several potential outcomes of that timeline. This was one of them. Call it a lucky guess … or maybe I'm just good at what I do. Either way, here I am." He opened his arms and grinned.

Bodhi glanced at Elena and shook his head. "Right. So, *why* are you here?"

"To help you, son. To redeem myself and right the wrongs I've caused. Clean my slate." He rose from Bodhi's easy chair and exposed his palms—his eyebrows lifted to a peak, and his eyes glistened. "The U.S. government confiscated the Mariner's Compass. Thank God you and Elena escaped with the other two relics."

Elena whispered to Bodhi, "Don't trust him, Corazón. How did he get here without the compass, huh?" She narrowed her eyes at Phillip and muttered, "Cabrón."

Bodhi nodded and whispered, "Good point." He turned toward Phillip, crossed his arms, and flexed his beefy biceps.

"So, the government confiscated the compass? Yet here you are. How'd you manage that? By being good at what you do?"

"I escaped through a crack in time. Their scientists forced me to open a portal using the compass ... and when I did, I seized the opportunity and jumped before they could stop me. I landed here ... been here a few days. Sorry, I cleaned out your fridge. I would have gone out to eat, but ... didn't want to miss your homecoming. I hope you don't mind."

Bodhi raised a brow and glanced at Elena. "That jives with the video we saw. He might be telling the truth."

"I'm not buying it," Elena hissed. "He's here for a reason, and it isn't a *good* reason. A clever viper doesn't waste its venom, Bodhi; it knows when to retract its fangs."

"Let's at least listen to what he has to say."

"Ay, Bodhi. That's like trusting a hawk with your chicken."

Phillip sighed and lowered his head. "I don't blame you for not trusting me. I've made a lot of mistakes in my life, son. I promise I'm only here to help ... to make up for years of—"

Elena threw up her hands and grumbled, "¡Venga! Spare us the fake tears. What do you want from us?"

Phillip paused. "Elena, I understand your anger and desire to protect my son. If you allow me to prove myself, you'll see I only want what's best for you. I want to help. The government is bent on finding all three relics to study, and we all know the consequences if that happens. We need each other … need to work together to secure the Trinity. With all three in our possession, we'll have the power to stop them."

Elena pointed a threatening finger. "No! The relics must be destroyed. They're a serious threat to our existence."

Phillip nodded. "Yeah, that's what I meant. Destroy them."

Elena scoffed and glared at Bodhi. "I can't listen to any more of his lies. We can't trust him, Bodhi."

Phillip cast a nervous glance toward Elena, then locked eyes with Bodhi. "Son, can we speak alone for a moment?"

Bodhi shook his head and wrapped his arm around Elena's shoulder. "Nah. Whatever you have to say, say it to both of us."

Phillip collapsed into the leather cushions of Bodhi's lounge chair. "Very well. Let me be straight with you. The government sent me here to find and take possession of the Tempus Glass and the timepiece."

Bodhi rolled his eyes and nodded. "Uh-hu. Now the truth comes out. You *are* a liar. So, what did they offer you?"

"Money. A lot of money. But more importantly, they promised to find my wife … your mother. I reassure you, I trust them less than you trust me."

Bodhi squatted on a loveseat next to Phillip. "And now we've come full circle and back to our original question. *Why are you here?*"

"I only want to find Ethel. That's why I'm here. I need your help, son. If we can retrieve the compass, I can locate Ethel … your mother. You can send us back in time, Bodhi … and never hear from me again. Do whatever you want with the relics. Use them … destroy them … rule the universe. I don't give a rat's ass. Nothing will matter once I have my Ethel. Please try to understand."

Bodhi lowered his head and exhaled a deep sigh. He locked eyes with Elena, her hands on her hips, glaring at him like a Catholic nun at boarding school, ready to whack his knuckles with a ruler. "Can we talk?" he asked.

Elena clapped a hand against her forehead. "Dios mío, Bodhi." She ambled toward the fireplace and straightened a photo of Gram on the mantle. "Sí ... let's talk outside."

Bodhi rose and turned toward Phillip. "Wait here."

Phillip pursed his lips, jutted his chin, then nodded. "Take your time. I'm not going anywhere."

Elena was the first out the front door. She stopped in the center of the porch and spun to face him, her head tilted with a cat-like glare.

"What are you doing, Corazón?" she whispered. "Are you seriously considering his story?"

Bodhi raised his palms and glanced toward the screen door. "Just ... just hear me out, okay?" keeping his voice low.

Elena rolled her eyes and huffed. She crossed her arms and leaned against a pillar near the porch stairs, continuing to glare at him.

"All right, Bodhi. I'm listening," she replied impatiently.

"Look, I don't trust him either. But I believe some of what he says."

"Which part?" she snapped back.

Bodhi raised his hands in a calming motion. "Sh. Keep it down, babe."

He continued. "The part about escaping through the vortex. We saw it ourselves when the agents showed us the video. That was *him*. Phillip was the guy who jumped."

"Okay, it was him. So, what ..."

"So, maybe the agents lied to us. What if they forced him to open the portal and jump?"

She shook her head. "I ... I don't understand your point."

"The agents made it seem like an unidentified man in their custody opened a portal and escaped, leaving the compass behind. I'm saying they left out a few facts when they visited us."

"What *facts*, Bodhi? You're making me crazy. What are you getting at?"

"They knew who he was. They lied to us. They bribed him to open the portal … to travel here and steal our relics from us. Meanwhile, they kept the compass as collateral to ensure he couldn't escape. The only way back to collect his reward would be the timepiece, the hourglass, or both."

Elena pinched the bridge of her nose and closed her eyes. "So, if he's telling the truth, why trust him? You're not making sense."

"I'm not saying we should trust him. I'm just saying that maybe we use him to steal the compass and destroy all three relics … and in the process, find my mother. Maybe using him is our best shot. Once we find her, we send them away … to be together and … I don't know … find their *happily ever after*."

"Oh, Bodhi … I don't believe him. He stole the relics once already. He'll try again. Never allow yourself to be bitten by the same snake twice." She pointed two fingers at her pupils. "Open your eyes, hombre."

She approached him and touched his cheek; her eyes softening. "What is going on inside this head of yours, Mi Amore?"

"I don't know … Maybe I should have helped him find my mom. Maybe *I* want to find my mom. Ask her why she abandoned me. I have so many questions for her, babe. Maybe all he wants is to find her and escape."

"No, Bodhi. He doesn't. He's lying, and he came here to steal the relics. Don't be a fool."

Bodhi pulled away from her and plopped onto the porch swing.

"I know he's lying, Elena. And I know he's a snake. But maybe with his help, we can recover the compass, find my mother, and I can finally have the chance to talk with her. We'll have the relics, and we can destroy them. We can send Phillip away and never hear from him again. It's a win-win."

Elena lowered her head and folded her hands in front of her. She inhaled an exasperated breath, stepped toward him, and kissed his cheek. She grasped both his hands and squeezed.

"You can't save everyone, Doctor Bodhi. Your parents mistreated and abandoned you when you were only a niño. You don't owe them a thing."

Bodhi rubbed his temples and clenched his jaw.

"Why did Gram separate them? She was the kindest, most loving woman I've ever known. Why would she do that?"

Elena sat next to him and rubbed his shoulders. "I don't think she meant to separate them, Bodhi. Sometimes, time travel is unpredictable in stressful situations. Bad things happen when we act in haste and without full control of our emotions. We both know this. I'm convinced these relics have spirits within them. Intelligence. Personalities."

"They're my parents, Elena. I know they were shitty parents, but I want to see my mother. Resolve some unfinished business. Wouldn't that be the right thing to do?"

"Vaya, Bodhi. How do you always see the stars hidden in the darkness?"

"Can we at least hear him out and listen to what he's proposing?" he asked.

"All right. We can listen. But I don't believe him, and I don't trust him. You're allowing your heart to outthink your brain, mi amigo."

He chuckled and patted her hand. "Elena always tells the truth. I need you to trust me."

"I *do* trust you, Bodhi. But I need to protect you from yourself sometimes … Ay. Let's hear what he has to say."

She rose and tugged at his hand.

Phillip sipped a glass of brandy and sucked the last drag from a cigarette, smashing the butt into a small glass bowl. Bodhi sat next to him as Phillip raised his glass and grinned. "Sorry. I helped myself to your stash. Wasn't sure how long you'd be. Here, I poured you one, son … Cheers."

Their glasses pinged. The brandy warmed Bodhi's throat and numbed his anxiety. Phillip set his drink on a small table. "So, what did you kids decide?"

Bodhi crinkled his brow and rubbed his beard. A twinge tightened his chest.

"Explain in detail how you plan to get the compass back and what you need from us."

Phillip leaned forward, his eyes darting from Bodhi to Elena and back. "Are you serious? You'll help me?"

"That depends on your plan," Bodhi said.

"The plan is simple. I know the exact location of the compass at a specific moment in time, and I need a ride back … to where I entered the vortex in the government's lab. I need the timepiece … or the Tempus Glass." He glanced at Elena, his tongue pressed against his cheek, and his eyes wild with excitement.

"We're not giving you either," Elena snapped.

"I don't expect you to. I only need a way back. Once we're there, you can freeze time, Elena … long enough for me to secure the compass. We return … you help me find Ethel and send us away, never to trouble you two love birds again."

Bodhi frowned and raised an eyebrow. "Let me get this straight. You want us to take you back to the point when you entered the portal to come here? That's it?"

"Exactly. Then, Elena uses the Tempus Glass to stop time. I grab the compass, and we leave. Simple as that."

Bodhi shook his head and wagged a finger. "Nah. I'll grab the compass."

"Okay. Sure. You grab the compass. The point is, we grab it and escape. It doesn't get much easier than that, son."

Bodhi locked eyes with Elena. Her worried glance softened.

"What do you think, Elena? Do we risk it?"

"My gut says no." She pointed a threatening finger. "If you betray us, Phillip, you'll regret your decision to come here."

"You have my word, Elena. I want the same thing as you … to see the relics destroyed. But not until I find my wife. Understood?"

Elena left the room and entered the bedroom. Phillip refilled Bodhi's glass of brandy. "One more drink together, son. Then we go make history." He winked. "See what I did there? Make history." He chuckled and sipped.

Elena returned, clutching the Tempus Glass. "Explain to me where we're going, Phillip."

He stood and extended his arm. "Take my hand, and you'll sense the echoes of where we're going. I'm still connected to the compass, which will lead us to the precise time and place we need to travel."

That last drink was strong—too strong. Bodhi's eyes blurred, and his head pounded. Phillip turned toward him, cocked his head, and grinned. "You okay, son? Eat something that didn't agree with ya?"

The words and Elena's shrills echoed inside Bodhi's head as if submerged under water. Bodhi leaped from his chair, stumbled to his knees, and face-planted on the rug as his world turned dark.

THREE

Shutters clapped against the beach house, as if annoyed by his slumber. Winds moaned through the cracks of the old home, hissing through the gaps in the window frames. Light rain pattered against the roof in rhythm with the gentle rolls of rumbling thunder.

Bodhi lifted his head, trying to focus and make sense of his blurred surroundings. He pushed himself off the wooden floor, landing on one knee, rubbing his throbbing temples, and steadying himself.

The beach house was dark—quiet—except for the droning rhythm of the rain pelting the windows.

"Elena," he whispered. "Elena? … Elena."

He leaped to his feet and stumbled forward, driving his shoulder into the wall to avoid hitting the floor again. "Elena!" he shouted, rushing into the bedroom, kitchen, and den. His voice grew hoarse and desperate.

"God, what have I done? You were right."

He buried his fist in the wall of his den. Crumbs of plasterboard exploded and fell like confetti across the floor. White dust covered his skinned and bloodied knuckles.

"Phillip! You son of a bitch." Bodhi wandered into the living room and squatted on the sofa, burying his face in his hands. *Where'd he take her? Damn it.*

Phillips's voice modulated within the howling winds. "She's not here, son. But I promise, she's safe. You seem to have this problem of losing the people you're supposed to protect … just saying."

Bodhi leaped from the sofa and charged Phillip. "I'll kill you—"

His body stiffened, suspended mid-stride, fists clenched. He couldn't move, couldn't speak, couldn't blink.

Phillip raised the Mariner's Compass in his right hand, opening a turbulent vortex behind him.

"I'm sorry it has to be this way, son. We wouldn't be at this juncture had you offered to help bring your mother back the first time I asked. But here we are … This is all your fault, you know." He clenched his teeth and scowled. "Where's the timepiece, Bodhi? I need all three or they won't help me find Ethel."

Phillip jammed a needle into the base of Bodhi's neck, then released him, watching him tumble to the ground. He kneeled next to him and snatched a handful of his T-shirt. "Where is it, boy? Where's the timepiece?"

"Go to hell."

"It doesn't have to be this difficult, Bodhi. All I want is to get my Ethel back, and I'll do whatever it takes to make that happen. Tell me where the timepiece is, and I'll take you to Elena."

"I don't have it. Find it yourself."

"You see … that's the problem. I can't. Echoes stopped emanating from the timepiece. Now, that could either mean you destroyed it or it's hidden, and the echoes are shielded. So, which is it?"

"You'll never find it. Gram made sure of it."

Phillip's eyes widened, and his lips curled into a smug grin. "Ah, the music box. Of course. You didn't destroy it. So, where have you hidden it?" He paced, his finger touching his temple. "Hm."

Phillip snapped his fingers, his eyes lit with elation. He pointed at Bodhi. "Cassie. You gave it to Cassie. Where is she, son?"

"Somewhere, you'll never find her. Know this, Phillip: I'm going to snap your neck like a cheap glow stick. That's a promise."

Phillip chuckled. "You might get that chance, and I'd probably deserve it. Tell me where the timepiece is, son. Don't force me to turn you over to the feds. They will do whatever they feel is necessary to force you to talk. Make it easy on yourself. You're still my son, and I don't want to see you suffer. I just want my wife … and I want to disappear."

"I thought that was our plan. We were going to make that happen."

"It requires the timepiece, son. You held out on me. Left me no choice."

Bodhi's eyelids grew heavy, and his body tingled; numbness tightened his neck into rolling knots. He lifted a quivering hand and flipped off Phillip before his arm fell limp.

Bodhi opened his eyes to a concrete ceiling and the annoying hum of a small air vent above him. He sat upright on a stiff canvas cot, planting his feet on a black-tiled floor. Four stainless steel walls surrounded him in an eight-by-ten holding cell that reeked of bleach. He glanced at a sturdy metal door to his right, noticing a small twelve-inch window secured with wired glass. An unfamiliar face glared at him through the glass as the tumblers clicked and rattled.

A tall, bald, muscular man of African descent entered the room— early forties, dressed in tan slacks, matted alligator shoes with no socks, and a white long-sleeved dress shirt, sleeves rolled up to his elbows. A short, squatty guard dressed in a gray uniform loomed in the doorway, holding a stun gun in one hand and a baton in the other.

The tall man narrowed his eyes and spoke with a slight West African accent. "Good morning, Doctor McMullin. I pray your stay has been pleasant so far, sir." He extended his hand. "Tyson Abara ... Agent Tyson Abara. They assigned your case to me. Is there anything I can get you? Some tea, a Coke perhaps?"

Bodhi ignored Abara's offer of a handshake. As he rose to face him, the guard placed a nervous hand on the stun gun and gripped his baton.

"Where's my wife?"

Abara placed a hand on Bodhi's shoulder. "I assure you, Doctor, she is fit and well cared for."

"I want to see her."

"In time ... in time. For now, I'm here to escort you to the café, where we can share an enjoyable chat and the finest government-issued breakfast you'll ever experience." He chuckled.

"The only *enjoyable* chat we need to share is the one where you allow my wife and me to go free."

"We shall discuss this in more detail over breakfast. Please ... follow me."

Bodhi walked side-by-side with Agent Abara down a long hallway toward an elevator, shadowed by the guard.

"What is this place?" Bodhi grumbled.

"This, sir, is a top-secret government installation. You are perfectly safe here, as is your wife."

Abara swiped a badge tethered to a lanyard around his neck across a sensor, opening an automatic door that led to an empty cafeteria. The two men loaded their trays with food and sat in a far corner.

His stomach rumbled from the savory scent of breakfast steak and hashed potatoes, as if he hadn't eaten in weeks.

"When can I see my wife?"

"Patience, Doctor. The reunion with your wife will occur after you've answered a few simple questions."

"Ask your questions," he mumbled as he sliced into his steak and squirted a zigzag pattern of ketchup over his hash browns.

"I will cut to the chase. We need to locate the timepiece, Doctor McMullin. Where is it?"

"In a place where you'll never find it."

Abara pushed his food tray aside and folded his hands. A crease formed across his rigid brow, and his coffee-colored eyes darkened. "That isn't a helpful answer, sir."

"But it *is* an answer …. So now that I've answered your question…"

Abara leaned toward Bodhi, his piercing gaze unsettling. Bodhi noticed the disjointed curve in the bridge of Abara's nose and a scar over his left brow. "Where can we find your daughter?"

"Why would I tell you that? Are you going to kidnap her, too? You can kiss my ass, Abara."

"I was hoping for a more pleasant and productive conversation, Doctor. However, it appears you've chosen to be uncooperative and rude … rather disappointing."

"What do you expect from me? You abduct my wife, lock me in a cell and you want to be cafeteria buddies … maybe have a couple beers afterward and shoot the shit? Do you have a wife, Agent? Children?"

He nodded. "Yes. Two sons."

"Do you care about their safety?"

"Of course."

"Then let my wife and I go. Return the hourglass to her. Destroy the compass, lock my father up, and throw away the key."

"I'm afraid I can't do that. These relics pose a high security threat to this country and the world. We need to contain them … to study them."

Bodhi slapped the table, widening Abara's stare. "To *weaponize* them, you mean."

"Our research will be in the best interest of our nation, I assure you."

Bodhi scoffed. "Oh, I'll sleep so much better tonight knowing that."

Abara steepled his fingers and sucked a deep breath. "Doctor, we need your help. You *and* your wife. We need to fully understand the power of these relics to know how to best safeguard them."

"The only way to safeguard them is to destroy them—to keep them out of the hands of people like you and my father."

"It's not that simple, I fear. We've observed the power of the compass but have only scratched the surface of its capabilities. We are on the precipice of understanding how the compass and the hourglass interact and how their combined energies multiply exponentially. Once we've secured the timepiece, the puzzle will be complete."

Bodhi shook his head and chuckled. "You have no idea what you're screwing around with. The power of these relics can destroy time and space as we know them. They could set off an implosion of the known universe and wipe us out of existence. You've heard of *The Big Bang*? Well, this would be the opposite of that, but worse."

Abara nodded and raised his brows. "You are making my point for me, Doctor … the very reason we need to take them out of your hands and put them into the hands of the most capable and educated scientists in the world to study." Abara pressed his palms together in a pretentious prayer. "Help us save humanity, Doctor McMullin. Before, we can't."

"I'm saving my family and yours, Agent Abara … by not."

Abara steepled his fingers and pressed them against his lips. His eyes narrowed, gazing through Bodhi's skull like a focused laser, cold and calculating.

"It is to my great displeasure that I must turn you over to our specialists, who will extract the truth from you, Bodhi. I beg you … do not force my hand. Tell me where we can recover the timepiece, and you and your family will be free to go. I guarantee your safety."

Bodhi leaned back in his chair, defiant and silent, crossing his arms and frowning.

Abara grimaced and nodded. "Very well, then. It's been a pleasure, sir."

He rose, tapped the guard on the shoulder, and muttered, "We're finished here. Take him to D.I."

Padded stainless steel cuffs bound his wrists to the arms of a lounge chair. His waist and ankles were also bound. A leather strap secured his head against the headrest—his face encased in a clear glass helmet. Headphones cupped his ears, and a silvery visor shielded his eyes. The surrounding walls appeared stark and bright.

"Doctor McMullin? Can you hear me? Are you there, Doctor?"

"Where am I? Who is this?"

"I'm your guide, Doctor. May I call you Bodhi?"

"Call me whatever you like. Just get me the hell out of here."

"Please relax, Bodhi. Listen to the sound of my voice and release your fears."

"Right. I'm strapped to the dentist chair from hell, and you want me to relax?"

"That's good. Humor is a nice first step, Bodhi."

"A first step for what? Let me out of here, damn it."

A robotic arm whirled and whizzed, rotating from beneath the chair like a serpent, injecting a needle into Bodhi's right thigh.

"What did you inject me with?"

"Focus on the sound of my voice, Bodhi. Open your mind and let go. Try not to fight it."

A flash of blinding white light enveloped his entire being, flooding him with warmth and an overwhelming sense of peace. He opened his eyes near a park. Children raced across a playground, scaling parallel bars, hanging off of twisted climbers, tumbling down slides, and bouncing on teeter-totters.

"Do you recognize it, Bodhi?"

He glanced to his left. A middle-aged man in a white smock, white-rimmed glasses, and wavy salt-and-pepper hair flashed an unnatural smile.

"What's happening to me? Who are you?"

"I told you ... I'm your guide, Bodhi. You may refer to me as Isaac."

Bodhi gasped; his heart raced the moment a young girl with curly blonde hair emerged from the slide into the sunlight.

"Blondie?"

"Do you remember this day, Bodhi?"

"Why am I here? Why are you showing me this?"

"This is a moment from your past. A moment in time you've never resolved." Isaac pointed towards a far bench. "You spent a lot of time on your cell phone in those days. More time developing your practice and finding a business partner than spending quality time with your daughter."

Bodhi's jaw dropped. His insides tightened. "This is the day I lost Cassie. Isn't it?"

Isaac tightened his lips and tilted his head. "There she goes. If only her father were paying more attention to her. So many children are abducted on playgrounds by bad players, Bodhi."

"Cassie ... Blondie?"

"Look how long it took you to notice her absence. You must have experienced quite the panic attack when you realized she was gone."

"No … no, Blondie," he whispered. Bodhi rushed after her before she could leave his sight. He gently grasped her elbow. Bouncy golden curls and satin blue eyes gazed up at him through a familiar, innocent smile. "Daddy?"

"I'm here, Blondie. You're safe, sweetheart."

"Why didn't you watch me, Daddy? Why did you lose me?" she cried.

"I-I didn't lose you, baby girl. We found you. I'm so sorry, sweetheart."

Bodhi dropped to one knee, pressed his hand against his pounding heart, and gasped. The sting of sweat blinded him. "Cassie? Blondie? Where are you, baby?" Darkness shrouded him. Old scars ripped open like flicks of a scalpel.

"I'm lost, Daddy. Where are you? Why did you leave me all by myself?"

"Stop it! This isn't real. Stop, please. I know this is bullshit! I only lost her for a couple of hours. We found her safe with one of the mothers in the park."

"We both know that isn't true, Bodhi. Maybe you insist on remembering it that way, but that's not what happened, now is it?"

"No. We found her." He pounded the ground with his fist.

"Her mother, your ex-wife, Savanna, found her at the precinct downtown. She'd been missing overnight. Wandering the streets all alone. Imagine her fear and the dangers she must have faced."

"I … I don't recall. We found her … she was safe."

"Your wife never forgave you, did she? Think of all the terrible scenarios that could have played out."

"Why are you doing this?"

"So, you can see the truth and accept it, Bodhi. The only way to mend unresolved trauma is to face it. Take accountability."

"I tried to find her. She disappeared so fast …" Tears spilled from his cheeks.

"It's okay, Bodhi. Thanks to her mother, Cassie was found safe and sound. She never trusted you with her daughter again. Isn't that right? In truth, you neglected your wife, Savanna, too. She moved on without you. Found a new love in your best friend, and closed the door on your marriage."

"Stop it. You know nothing about me or my family."

"Aw, but *you* do, Bodhi. These are *your* suppressed thoughts, *your* hidden memories, we are extracting. The real ones, not the ones you've created in your mind to protect yourself … to continue the lie you've told yourself all these years."

"I want out of here … Now! Where's my wife? I want to see Elena!"

"Where is Cassie, Bodhi? Where have you abandoned her now?"

Bodhi rose and clenched his jaw. "I'll never tell you. Do whatever you want with me; you'll never find her. This mind game you're playing will not work, you sick bastards."

"Your heart was in the right place, Bodhi. But how many times have you failed, Cassie? You divorced her mother. Took away the only home she ever knew. Do you know how she suffered?"

Seventeen-year-old Cassie screamed into her pillow; her wails pulsated through his heart and soul like a jackhammer.

"Daddy! Come back … I can't do this without you. I miss you so, so much, Dad. Why would you leave me?"

"You broke her heart, Bodhi. Why would you do that?"

"Her mother divorced me, damn it. I never wanted it …"

"But you abandoned Cassie. You left and never told her why."

"I had to move out. She understood that."

"Did she? She needed you, and you weren't there for her in her most vulnerable moments. Your job was to protect her, and you failed."

"Enough … please. No more."

"Where is Cassie, Bodhi? She needs you right now. Tell us where she is, and we'll bring her to you."

"Do you think I'm some kind of idiot? I told you. Your head games won't work. Cassie is safe and you'll never find her, you sons of bitches."

"Where is the timepiece, Bodhi? Give us the timepiece, and you, Cassie, and Elena can go home and return to your lives."

"Go to hell."

An electric charge surged through every nerve in his body, as if boiling bone marrow and exploding blood vessels. His moans became semi-paralyzed grunts.

"Where's the timepiece, Bodhi? Is it in Cassie's possession?"

"Torture me, kill me. I'll never give up my daughter," he cried.

A gray fog engulfed him and opened a scene from Gram's beach house. Gram was arguing with Phillip and another woman—he couldn't make out the conversation. A small boy peered from behind the door of the bedroom. Bodhi stepped closer.

"Give us our son, Mom. Give him up right now, or we'll take him."

Gram looks so young, he thought.

"You don't deserve my James. He's a good boy, and you've abused and abandoned him repeatedly. Get out of my house, Phillip. Take your drug-addicted wife with you. I won't allow you to ruin his life. He deserves better … he deserves a chance in life with someone who loves him."

"The court said he's ours. Give me my son, Mom. I won't ask again."

Gram raised the timepiece and chanted, suspending Phillip and Ethel in time like a video on pause. A roaring vortex burst into existence from nothing, inhaling the couple into its whirring and glimmering core. In an instant, the vortex fizzled, and silence dominated the room.

"Look what you're responsible for, Bodhi. Your grandmother banished your parents into oblivion and separated them in time. Rather cruel, don't you think? They may have been terrible parents, but did they deserve this? All because of you, Bodhi. Your grandmother abused the timepiece and used it for evil. We must retrieve it so this kind of malpractice can never recur."

"My grandmother was protecting me. The same way I'm protecting my daughter. Go screw yourselves. That woman was a saint."

"Where is the timepiece, Bodhi? Where is Cassie?"

"Safe from you."

"This is regrettable, Bodhi," Isaac said. "Initiate level two."

Jolts of electricity coursed through his body in three-second intervals, each growing stronger. Bodhi tensed and cried out. The shocks continued.

"Where is the timepiece, Bodhi?"

He gritted his teeth and writhed in the chair, bellowing.

"Kiss my ass!" he shrieked.

"Initiate level three..."

FOUR

Cassie sat upright in the blackness of her bedroom and inhaled a screech—her moist nightgown clung to her trembling body.

A warm, comforting hand massaged her shoulder blades, and muscular arms embraced her from behind.

"Bad dream?"

The drone of William's gentle voice cut through the silence and slowed her racing heart.

"I … I was dreaming about my dad. Something's wrong. He was in pain, trapped somewhere dark. I felt him crying out for me. It's so weird."

Tears streamed down her cheeks. She lay back on her pillow and glanced toward the outline of William's face in the night.

"I'm sure it was all a terrible dream, Cassie. How about I make you a nice hot cup of cocoa, doll?"

She caressed his cheek and kissed his lips. "Why are you so good to me, Cappie? How did I get so lucky?"

"Because of thoughts like that, darl'n. Don't move, I'll be right back."

William flipped on a small brass lamp beside the bed and slipped through the dim light into the kitchen. An uneasiness persisted and tormented her. What if her dad was in trouble and needed her? The dream seemed so real.

"Here you go, gal. Careful, don't scald your tongue."

Cassie wrinkled her brow and glared at him. "Seriously? Two lonely little marshmallows in a vast ocean of cocoa?"

He grinned as he tossed her the entire bag.

"William? What should I do?"

"I think you should drink your cocoa, lay off the marshmallows, and fall back asleep. Let's talk about your dream tomorrow … if you even remember it."

William switched off the lamp and rolled over, wrapping himself in the blankets and yanking them away from Cassie, leaving her exposed to the cool night air. She set her empty cup on her nightstand and poked him in the shoulder.

"Hey … hey you. You stole all the covers. Hello?"

Deep breaths transformed into nasal snores. She swatted his arm with the bag of marshmallows and huffed. He snorted and mumbled, "What?"

"You're hogging the covers, dude."

Whimpers turned to whining, and whining turned to wailing. The baby was awake.

Cassie nudged William. "Hey. Hey buddy. It's your turn. Your son is calling you."

He snorted, then snored in a deep, relaxed rhythm.

She flung the covers. "Ugh. Really? I take back what I said."

Cassie padded across the floor, pulling her silken robe snug around her shoulders. William mumbled, "You're the best …" Snores resumed.

She warmed a bottle of milk and patted Little William back to sleep, but her nightmare continued to nag at her. The thought of her daddy in pain tightened her throat and had her insides twisting in knots. Cassie opened the pantry and slid several canned goods to the side. She removed a key from an empty can of green beans and opened a hidden panel on the pantry wall. Reaching inside, she grasped Gram's music box.

34

Cassie set the box in the center of the kitchen table and stared at it for over a minute. She inhaled a deep sigh and lifted the lid, removing the timepiece and setting it on the table. She cupped the relic in both hands and stared at it. Closing her eyes, she focused on the soft vibrations and faint echoes emanating from its shiny case.

Visions of her dad strapped to a chair and suffering flooded her mind. She witnessed his misery and sensed his anguish.

"Daddy? What are they doing to you?" she whispered.

Cassie pulled on a pair of jeans, slipped into her lucky powder-blue UCLA hoodie Bodhi gave her years ago, and tucked her feet into a pair of sneakers. She loaded a Walther PP .32 caliber pistol and slipped it into the kangaroo pocket of her hoodie. The handgun was a wedding gift from her best friend Rita. She's never fired it.

She wrote William a note and tucked the corner beneath a ceramic bowl filled with scarlet mountain apples on the kitchen counter.

Dear William,

Please forgive me, sweetheart. The nightmare was real. Call Rita if you need help with the baby. I promise I'll be back soon, Cappie! Try not to worry, and don't eat my marshmallows.

All my love, Cass

The vibrations increased as she vocalized on their pitch. A vortex exploded into a burst of colors like a three-dimensional kaleidoscope on LSD. She concentrated all her love and energy on her dad and leaped into its terrifying jaws, tumbling into a vast, timeless darkness.

FIVE

Bodhi shivered, stretched across the cold metal-framed cot of his cramped stainless-steel prison. He bunched a wool khaki blanket around his shoulders and squeezed his eyes shut. Beads of sweat dribbled from his temples like condensation on a cold window pane. His joints ached, as if dislocated and rammed back into place countless times, and his eyes throbbed. He once took a blind shot to the crown of his helmet in the waning minutes of a game against Arizona State, which sent him crumbling to the turf like a condemned building. This was a lot like that.

The painful visions his tormenters induced of young Cassie continued to afflict him—their cruelty honed towards his heart with the precision of a laser-tipped arrow. It broke him. The truth he'd denied all these years came flooding back. Cassie wasn't gone for a few hours; she was gone the entire night, and he struggled to suppress his sobs.

A faint whisper echoed through the darkness like the soft rustle of an evening breeze. "Daddy?"

Bodhi clamped his palms over his ears and cried out. "No more … please. I'm sorry, Cass! God, I'm so sorry, baby." He quivered and tugged the blanket snug beneath his chin.

Soft fingers cradled his face. "Daddy? It's me … Cassie."

"No. You're not real," his gravelly voice fading.

36

Gentle hands gripped his collar. "Dad. Wake up. I'm here to take you home."

Cassie's blurred face materialized in the dim light, framed by a powder-blue hoodie.

"Blondie? How did you—"

Cassie slipped the timepiece from her pocket. She grinned like when she was twelve after stealing his stethoscope to listen to her stomach growl.

"I heard you. Somehow, I knew you were in trouble. So, I'm here, Daddy. It's my turn to be the hero and rescue you … yay." She politely clapped her hands.

He scrambled to his feet and took her by the hand. "Cass … it's a trap. Now I see their plan … Torture me to lure you here."

Cassie's face turned ashen. "Maybe we should go. Where's Elena?"

"I don't know. The bastards won't tell me. But you can bet they already know *you're* here. Get out of here, Cass. Before it's too late. I'll be alright. Don't worry about me."

"Come with me, Dad."

"I can't leave without Elena. You need to get back to your family and secure the timepiece. Go."

The crackle of a speaker scratched the chilled air like ripped Velcro. "I'm afraid it's too late, Doctor. You and your daughter are safe as long as you stay put and don't do anything brash. I'll be in momentarily. Please have a seat next to your father, Cassie. So glad you could join us."

"Give me the timepiece," Bodhi whispered.

She slipped it into his palm like drug money.

"Hold my hand, Blondie, and don't ask questions … just trust me."

Her eyes widened, darting from his stoic glare to the steel door and back. She muttered like a ventriloquist, moving only her eyes. "What are you going to do? … Dad?"

He pressed his index finger to his lips. "Sh. No questions, Cass."

37

Tumblers clinked, and the heavy metal door swung wide.

Bodhi moved the hands of the timepiece ahead one minute and concentrated his energy. Agent Abara entered the room and froze like a faulty laptop.

"Let's go, Cass … now."

Bodhi and Cassie slipped past Abara into the empty concrete hallway illuminated by an endless row of flickering neon rods.

"Dad, what the heck was that? Why did everything stop?"

"A time loop … only temporary though … we gotta work fast to find Elena."

"How do we do that?"

"The Tempus Glass. I'm already tracking the echoes; once we have it, we can locate her."

The echoes led them up three flights of stairs into a lab. Behind a row of bulletproof glass windows, the Tempus Glass rested upon a crystal pedestal protected by an intricate web of green lasers within a ten-by-fifteen-foot room.

"Um, Dad?"

"I know, I know … I think we're screwed."

The trudging of boots echoing in the stairwell behind them set his heart pounding.

"We have to go, Blondie."

"But what about Elena?"

"I'll come back for her. Hold my hand."

The roar of a vortex swallowed them, opening a window to December 15, 1942, inside her beach home in Hawaii—the same day she left to rescue him.

Bodhi gripped Cassie's shoulders and kissed her on the forehead.

"Blondie, I need to tell you something, sweetheart … something I should have told you years ago. I've been in denial for so long, and have to get this off my chest."

"What's wrong, Dad?"

"Cass, I'm so sorry I lost you in the park … when you were little. I-I left the house when Mom wanted me out … when I should have—" His shoulders quivered as he fought back his sobs.

"Oh, my God … Dad. What are you talking about? I don't remember being lost. Mom picked me up." She caressed his cheek—her eyes grew misty and widened.

"I let you down, Cass. And I'm sorry."

"Aw, Daddy. Everything's okay now. I've got *your* back this time."

He squeezed her tightly, unable to let go.

She grunted. "Uh, Dad … you're crushing me."

He inhaled a deep breath and sighed. "I'll see you soon, Blondie. I promise."

Her eyes misted. "You better."

Bodhi turned away and concentrated on the timepiece until a soft hand gripped his elbow. "I love you so much, Daddy. Please, please, be careful." She sniffled, wiped her eyes with her palms, and put on a brave smile.

Cassie placed the pistol in his hands and nodded.

"No, Cass. Hang on to this … and don't hesitate to use it."

Bodhi opened a spiraling vortex, dove headfirst into its jaws, and disappeared. He tumbled through an endless vacuum of black eternity, concentrating on the lab where he had located the Tempus Glass—his only shot at finding Elena.

Bodhi stepped through the vortex and entered the room next to the Tempus Glass, nearly compromising the green laser grid. Three armed soldiers outside the window scrambled to unlock the door, one raising a rifle and focusing a red dot directly on his forehead.

Time froze as the hands of the timepiece locked into place. Green laser beams surrounding the Tempus Glass dissipated into a green atomic cloud. Bodhi wasted no time snatching the relic from its perch and turned his attention to the hum modulating between the timepiece and the hourglass.

In an instant, Bodhi passed through concrete and stainless steel into an eight-by-ten cell. Elena was curled in a fetal position on a canvas cot in the center of the space, her body quivering with quiet sobs.

"Elena," he whispered. She jerked from his touch.

A shriek vibrated off the compressed walls, and she scurried like a frightened kitten to a shadowy corner and cried, "Stay away from me!"

"Hey … it's me, sweetheart. It's okay. It's your turn to buy dinner, beautiful. I'm here to pick you up. Am I too early?"

Moist, reddened eyes covered by oily strands of curls gazed at him like a battered and frightened child. Her voice quivered with a nervous titter. "Bodhi?"

Elena leaped from the floor straight into his arms, clinging to his neck and burying her face in his chest. "You came for me … I knew you would. I knew it. I prayed to the Blessed Virgin over and over." She sniffled and wiped her tears. A joyful, innocent whimper escaped her throat. Bodhi presented the Tempus Glass like a trophy and tilted his head, raising his eyebrows. "Time to go, princess."

Elena's eyes widened. She clutched the hourglass while Bodhi gripped the timepiece as they squeezed each other's hands. "Where should we go, Corazón? Quickly … we need to run."

"I don't know … maybe Palm Springs for a round of golf, or Santa Fe for some night skiing. How about the '76 Rose Bowl, where UCLA thumped unbeaten Ohio State?"

"Bodhi! Dios mío … use your brain, not your jokes."

"Sorry. Let's go to New York. Nineteen-forty. The World's Fair. I'll buy you the most amazing ice cream cone you—"

The cell door crashing against the wall sent a jolt of adrenaline coursing through his veins. They stammered backwards.

"I can't believe you made it this far, son. I'm sort of proud of you. Now, hand over the relics." He outstretched his arm and wriggled his fingers.

Phillip raised the Mariner's Compass and glared at them with a heinous grin that curled the corners of his lips like a comic book villain. A bright magenta fog emanated from the compass, filling the room and sending Bodhi and Elena into a time loop of the past twenty seconds. Elena activated the Time Freeze power of the Tempus Glass, halting the loop mid-cycle. Together, they stepped between moments, becoming invisible and undetectable to Phillip. A golden orb the size of a golf ball hovered over the Mariner's Compass with strands of pure white light connecting the repeating events of the loop.

"Look, Bodhi. The door crashing into the wall is the reset point for the time loop. We need to put our brains together and stop it."

"We've got to sever those strings," he said.

Elena used the hourglass to shift the timing of the door crash. Threads of light connected to the orb quickly frayed, dissolving the loop with spiraling crackles and pops like the dying fizzle of a firecracker. Phillip crashed against the wall.

He shook his head and stretched his jaw. "Man, I guess I underestimated you two. I need those relics, son. I'm sorry."

Phillip shrugged and exposed his palms. "There's no way out. You and Elena need to cooperate. It's the only way I can get back to Ethel."

"What happened to teaming up to destroy the relics?"

Phillip grimaced and cocked his head. "The situation changed. Now, hand them over. I don't want to see you get hurt, Bodhi. You can return to your lives, and this will all be over. Go back to being a family with Elena and Cassie. Think about *them* for a minute."

Elena scowled. "I knew you were a lying snake. Hand over the compass, and we'll spare your life."

"I didn't want it to go down this way," Phillip said with a frown. "We could have worked together to save your mother. If you won't cooperate, then you leave me no choice."

Phillip spun the compass needle, creating a deafening screech. The sands of the Tempus Glass flared into a burst of emerald light so bright it seared their eyes, dropping them to their knees. The hourglass ignited in her hand like a torch, scorching her with waves of electricity. She shrilled and dropped the relic.

Phillip stepped toward Elena to claim his prize and turn both relics against Bodhi.

"Neither one of you understands the power of these relics. They're beyond your abilities. Only I understand them."

Phillip adjusted the compass needle, intensifying the electrical current pouring from the hourglass. Light flashed like ball lightning from the timepiece, singing Bodhi's palm.

"We're done here. Time to give them up," Phillip demanded.

Elena grasped Bodhi's wrist and screeched, "Grab the timepiece, Bodhi!"

He palmed the timepiece, frying his hand like the touch of a hot lightbulb—burning flesh filling his nostrils. Elena seized the Tempus Glass and raised the relic toward Phillip, warbling a majestic song like the cry of a dying nightingale.

The Tempus Glass crackled and discharged an emerald lightning bolt into the timepiece, locking them in sync and setting off an array of dazzling shimmers that formed a radiant shield around Bodhi and Elena. Seconds later, it detonated, sending Phillip crashing into the wall, dazed and confused.

Phillip's eyes widened, his mouth agape, struggling to speak. "What the hell did you do?" he mumbled.

Soldiers poured into the cell like cockroaches, securing the compass and dragging Phillip into the hallway.

"Stay where you are!" one soldier hollered.

Elena squeezed Bodhi's hand and closed her eyes. The roar of a jet engine filled the room as a terrible vortex ripped a gash in time and space.

Soldiers fired a spray of bullets, lodging in the shield, then falling harmlessly to the floor in a wave of tiny pings. Bodhi and Elena locked elbows and leaped into the raging cyclone as it fizzled and closed behind them, headed toward a dark and unknown destination.

SIX

Bodhi and Elena stepped into a luxurious stateroom enveloped by the warm glow of a brass chandelier. The chandelier's crystal pendants scattered a vibrant rainbow of glitter across the glossy reddish-brown mahogany walls. Intricate inlays of lighter wood formed delicate floral patterns along the edges of the panels. Above the wainscoting, the wallpaper was a soft cream damask, its pattern subtle yet elegant, lending an air of sophistication to the space. A faint but pleasant scent of polished wood and lavender lingered, and the floor vibrated beneath them from the roar of a powerful engine.

A four-poster bed dominated the room, draped with heavy brocade curtains in a deep burgundy and trimmed with golden tassels. The plush mattress was topped with a white linen duvet edged with lace and adorned with an array of embroidered silk cushions. A delicately laced canopy was suspended above the bed.

An ornately carved writing desk stood beneath a circular porthole at the far end of the cabin, allowing a glimpse of the vast ocean beyond. The desk had a matching chair with velvet upholstery; its legs curved gracefully, like the paws of a lion. The surface of the desk was cluttered with essentials: a crystal inkwell, monogrammed stationery, and a small silver clock ticking softly, the hands positioned at half-past eleven.

Across from the bed, a marble-topped dresser supported a tall oval mirror framed in gold leaf. A silver tray rested atop the dresser, holding a decanter of brandy, two crystal tumblers, and a small vase of fresh-cut roses. Next to it, a matching wardrobe with gilded handles was filled with tailored suits and elegant gowns.

"Bodhi, where are we?" she whispered.

"No clue. Seems we're stowaways in somebody's first-class cabin."

Elena padded toward the porthole. "Dios mío, we're in the middle of the sea. Why does it look so big?" She made the sign of the Cross and mumbled a prayer.

"Yeah. We might want to slide out of here before the occupants return." He grasped her hand and tugged her toward the door. She pulled against him, crinkled her brow, and ogled him from head to toe.

"This décor isn't your time or mine. And look how we're dressed? We have to blend in with the era, hombre."

"How do we do that?"

She pointed at the wardrobe.

He raised an eyebrow and scoffed. "Steal their clothes? None of those suits is going to fit me." He fanned his arms. "I have like a nine-foot wingspan."

"We have to try," she insisted.

Elena allowed her white cotton dress to fall around her ankles. She stepped out of the dress and slipped on an elegant sapphire silken gown with a soft V-neckline framed in delicate lace. Then she slid her feet into matching satin pumps and styled her hair into an intricate updo pinned with a sapphire-and-diamond comb. She slipped the Tempus Glass inside a matching purse and sighed as she gazed at herself in the mirror.

"Damn … you look hot, babe," he said with wandering eyes.

Elena grinned and posed. She glanced up at him through her reflection and cast a sultry gaze. "You think so?"

"Trust me. You do."

She spun and grabbed him by the wrist. "Get dressed, amigo. We need to go. Vámonos."

Bodhi did his best to slip into a black Edwardian suit. The pants fit, but were three inches high at the ankle. The seams of the dress shirt and black vest stretched to the point of nearly tearing, and he curled his size-eleven feet into a size-ten pair of black leather shoes. His timepiece blended well, clipped to the vest.

"This jacket won't work. Help me take it off. I'll carry it over my shoulder."

He glanced in the mirror and chuckled. "I look like an overstuffed mattress trying to squeeze into a pillowcase."

"Ooh la la, Bodhi," she chuckled, "You look handsome and charming. Now, vamos."

As they shuffled towards the exit, the doorknob rattled, and a key scraped inside the slot. Bodhi clutched her wrist and pulled her toward the bed, both scurrying beneath it.

He pressed his index finger to his lips. Elena blinked rapidly as her eyes widened like chestnut orbs.

"Grab your trunks and a bath towel, luv. I want to relax by the pool."

"Oh, and how you fancy your swimsuit, darling. Wiggling your little tushy for the crew and every handsome bloke you pass."

"I do no such thing. I do not appreciate these unfounded and unceasing accusations, Walter. If that is your attitude, you may wait in the cabin while I bathe. Not to worry ... I will return in time for tea."

"Please go with her, Walter," Bodhi whispered.

The man inhaled a deep nasally breath. "I shall accompany you, my dear. I shan't have you bathing by the pool unattended."

She huffed exasperated. "Ugh. Have it your way, Walter. Have it your way. Make yourself useful and fetch my sunglasses from the desk, will you, dear?"

After the click of the latch and the slam of the door, they exhaled in unison.

"I'll bet Walter follows her to the bathroom and waits outside the door for her to finish," he chuckled.

"Huy, Bodhi. I could never tolerate such a jealous, smothering, weak-minded man."

"Let's get the hell out of here. See if we can figure out where we are," he said.

They slipped into an elegant hallway, the walls covered in polished pearl-white wooden panels with crown molding running along the ceiling. Mahogany handrails lined the walls on either side, supported by shiny nickel brackets.

The hallway led to an elevator. Like everything else on the vessel, the elevator screamed of Edwardian luxury. Wrought-iron gates adorned with intricate floral and scroll motifs and crowned with decorative crests. Soft light from a windowed ceiling showered the polished brass with glittery accents.

A lustrous marble floor framed the landing with a diamond-patterned inlay and black tiles that contrasted with the white. Fluted Corinthian columns framed the elevator, adding a timeless, lavishness to the setting.

"Bodhi, this place looks like a wealthy palacio. Everything is … muy elegante. It steals my breath."

"No doubt. The style, the era … We're definitely squatters on an ocean liner of luxury. But which one? And what year is it?"

The wrought-iron gates slid open. An elevator attendant stepped onto the landing dressed in a crisp black uniform adorned with silver buttons

and matching epaulets. A glossy-brimmed cap sat neatly atop his immaculately groomed sandy-blonde hair.

His double-breasted jacket displayed a small embroidered crest. The crest was of a golden lion standing on its hind legs, encircled by golden laurel leaves. A majestic crown sat atop the lion, adorned with jewels.

"Good day, Madam." He nodded towards Bodhi. "Good day, Sir. May I take you to your desired floor?" he asked in a polished British accent.

"Yes, please take us to the main deck."

"Very good, sir. Step inside, and I will escort you to *A Deck*."

Elena gripped Bodhi's elbow as the elevator rose and rattled. Bodhi pointed at the crest on the attendant's jacket.

"That's an interesting logo. What does it represent?"

The man frowned and glanced at his jacket as if he had a stain. He narrowed his eyes and furrowed his brow. "Well, Sir, this is the insignia of the Cunard Line."

"Cunard Line? That's a British cruise line company."

The attendant raised a curious eyebrow. "Correct, Sir."

"And of course, this ship is one of its ocean liners."

"Yes, Sir."

"And would this be the ... Titanic, maybe?"

The man snickered. "No, Sir. Titanic was a member of the White Star fleet. You Americans have a jolly good sense of humor. Tragedy about the Titanic, though."

"Uh ... yes. Huge tragedy. Especially the part where Rose promised Jack she'll never let go ... What does she do? She lets go."

"I'm sorry, Sir. I don't follow."

"Ah, never mind. Dumb joke. It seems like only yesterday when the Titanic sank, huh, buddy?" He turned towards Elena and winked, cocky in his approach of questioning the attendant.

"Indeed, Sir."

"And how long has it been? Time flies when you're cruising."

"Three years, sadly."

He glanced at Elena and lowered his brow. He muttered, "It must be nineteen-fifteen."

"This is your floor, Sir … Madam."

Bodhi allowed Elena to step off first. He paused and rested his hand on the attendant's shoulder. "This ship isn't going to sink, is it?"

He chuckled. "I would hardly think so, old chap. However, there are rumblings of German U-boats targeting passenger ships. But not to worry. We can outrun any U-boat with ambitions to make a name for itself."

"Now, that's interesting," Bodhi mumbled.

"If you'll pardon me, Sir, there are passengers behind you attempting to step aboard the elevator. Have a pleasant day."

Bodhi turned to intercept the indignant glares of a finely dressed family. He stepped aside and extended his elbow to Elena.

"Ay, Bodhi. Your conversation was suspicious and clumsy. You're going to get us arrested if you're not careful. Why not ask him the name of the ship and be done with it?"

He pressed his tongue to his cheek and raised an eyebrow. "And asking the name of the ship wouldn't sound suspicious?"

"No. Watch me."

Elena stopped a trio of young ladies on a stroll, giggling and having a pleasant conversation.

"Señoritas? I love your umbrellas."

They glanced at each other and rolled their eyes.

"Can I ask the name of this ship?"

The young ladies tittered and scurried around her. One girl whispered something in French and glanced back at Elena.

Bodhi leaned against the ship's rail, arms crossed, hair blowing in the warm breeze, head tilted, flashing an overblown smirk.

"Well, that panned out nicely. What'd they say?"

"Huy, Señor. Unfortunately, I don't speak French." She slapped his arm as he snickered and covered up like a boxer.

"Well, there's no need to learn French, sweetheart." He pointed towards a lifeboat secured to the side of the ship.

She squinted and whispered, "RMS Lusitania?"

"Yeah. We're in big trouble. Not sure why we're here."

"Why? Why are we in trouble?"

"Remember the U-boats the elevator guy mentioned? The Lusitania was plugged by a torpedo in May of nineteen-fifteen. Not sure of the exact date, but here we are." He raised his palm. "High five."

He exaggerated a glance around the ship and slung his jacket over his shoulder. "Feels like May, doesn't it?"

"Bodhi, what's a U-boat?"

"Let's grab a coffee and a croissant, and I'll tell you all about U-boats, and torpedoes—maybe find a newspaper with today's date. I meant to ask. Can you swim?"

SEVEN

Elena sipped a black cup of coffee while Bodhi nibbled on a ham and Swiss croissant at the Verdanah Café, overlooking a vast, sleepy ocean. A warm, salty breeze wafted through the outdoor café, adding to the peacefulness of the moment. A gentleman at a nearby table finished a cup of tea and rolled up a newspaper, catching Bodhi's eye. The second he slid his chair away from the table and rose, Bodhi tapped his arm and pointed at the paper.

"Pardon me, Sir. May I have that?"

The man tipped his derby and plopped the tabloid on their table. Before he could leave, Bodhi scanned the date: *May 1, 1915*.

"Sir? How old is this newspaper?"

"Six days. Picked it up in New York. Hadn't read it till now. The news is all foul these days. Pleasant day, old boy."

Bodhi glanced at Elena and tapped his finger beneath the date at the top of the front page. "This means today is May seventh. Now, I may be mistaken, but I believe the Lusitania was torpedoed a few miles off the coast of Ireland … Thank God we don't see a coast."

Elena frowned. "We should leave. I don't know why we're here."

Across the café, a woman scribbling in a brown leather sketchbook drew his curiosity. Is she a journalist or a celebrity of the day, maybe? She seemed out of place, but eerily familiar.

Tall and poised—an Audrey Hepburn type. Long, dark hair, frayed but pulled into a neat updo. Her wardrobe was simple. A plain mauve summer dress and flat sandals. No makeup or nail polish. Pale skin, legs crossed, and shoulders slouched. His attraction to her confounded him.

The woman glanced up from her journal, her haggard eyes filled with anguish. They narrowed the moment she caught his stare. The intensity of her gaze struck him, reflected in her vibrant aquamarine eyes, almost mystical, like a sea witch.

She folded her sketchbook, scampered past their table, and disappeared into the growing crowd.

A soft touch caressed his forearm. "What's wrong, Cariño? You have the eyes of a spooked horse."

"That woman … she seemed out of place … but … there's something familiar about her, and I can't put my finger on it."

"I think you are … as you say … paranoid."

"I'm not paranoid. Just a little weirded out at the moment. And I don't know why." He shrugged and forced a quick smile. "Maybe it's nothing."

She touched his chin and directed his stare towards her. "Take me for a walk. Hold my hand and tell me how much you love me. I didn't get the chance to thank you for saving me, Mi Amore."

She slid her fingers over his knuckles and gently squeezed his hand. "Thank you," she whispered, the warmth of her kiss against his knuckles raising the hairs on his forearm.

The devotion in her gaze was a reminder of the devastation he would know if he ever lost her.

"You're welcome." Bodhi folded his hands and returned her gaze. Emotions overwhelmed him, smitten by her beauty and the irresistible charm that had stolen his heart years ago. He glided his fingertips over the contours of her proud jawline.

"I had a lifetime of heartbreak before I met you, Elena. You've taught me everything I know about love, and I'd be lost without you, sweetheart … like a seagull without a coast … a ship without a captain."

She rested her palm over her heart and sighed. "Oh, Corazón, it's been too long since you've spoken such things to me. I have chills up my arms, and I want to cry. You rescued my heart, and I love you with every piece of it. I fail to tell you how deep my love burns for you." Her voice lowered. "I would die for you, Mi Amore."

Bodhi sucked a breath and swallowed. "Ugh. I think this ship is getting to us. Hey, isn't that Celine Dion over there?"

She turned to look and crinkled her brow. "Where? Who is this Celine Dion person?"

"Never mind … it's a dumb joke. You know I tell jokes when I'm nervous. Bad habit."

Elena lowered her head and raised a sultry glance. A lock of hair fell over her left eye, and her breathing intensified. "Make love to me, Corazón—wild, crazy love. Take me … take me right now. I cannot wait another second. The sound of your voice … the way that you are looking at me is pure torture. I crave your kiss on my neck and your body inside of mine."

"Whoa…" Bodhi rose and grabbed her by the hand, leading her out of the café and onto the deck. They scurried past rows of lifeboats, pausing momentarily, glancing in both directions. "I have an idea."

A whimper rose in her throat. "I love your ideas. Tell me."

Bodhi raised the canvas of lifeboat #16 and lifted Elena inside, ensuring they wouldn't be spotted. He closed the flap as an older couple strolled past. The woman flashed a suspicious glance and scoffed. Once they passed, he joined Elena beneath the neon blue skies and the scent of warmed canvas.

Bodhi peered through a slit in the canvas until he was sure the coast was clear. He swung his leg over the side of the lifeboat and leaped onto the deck with a thump—the cool breeze sent shivers through his moist dress shirt, which he quickly buttoned. Elena outstretched her arms, falling into his grasp as he swung her in a half-circle and landed her on the wooden deck, her hair disheveled and her dress wrinkled and pulled sideways. She rested her hand over her breast and sighed, as he dabbed the sweat from her brow and chuckled.

"I need to catch my breath, you beastly man. What will I ever do with you? You're a savage and have ravished me once again."

"I'm beginning to question who's doing the ravishing here," he muttered.

A small voice with a gentle Irish accent interrupted their moment. "What were da two of ya doing inside that lifeboat? Are ya stowaways?"

Bodhi craned his neck toward the voice and glanced downward into the twinkling gray-blue eyes of a twelve-year-old girl, smirking as if she had a big secret. She wore a cream pinafore-like dress trimmed with lace and embroidery, sturdy brown leather boots, and a rounded straw hat. In her right hand, she gripped a colorful lollipop like a reporter's microphone.

Bodhi stammered. "Uh, we were just inspecting the inside of this lifeboat. We're inspectors. We wanted to make sure you and your family are safe in case of an emergency."

Elena giggled. "What's your name, Mija?"

"Josie. Josie Quin. Ya don't look like inspectors, ya know. I mean, yer not dressed like it."

Bodhi playfully frowned and glanced at Elena. "We're undercover, Josie. Trying not to draw attention to ourselves. That way, nobody will wonder what we're doing, and we won't create a panic. You don't want to create a panic, do you?"

"Heavens no. So, are ya going to inspect the other boats, too?"

"Of course … Sure."

"Well, ya better git to it. It took ya long enough to inspect that one."

"Uh … you're right. We should get to it, and you should probably go find your parents."

Josie tugged at her auburn curls—the corners of her strawberry lips turned downward. "My Papa died two years ago, and my mum is waiting fer me in Liverpool."

Elena knelt in front of her. "You're all alone on this ship, Mija?"

She tapped the deck with her boot. "I'm traveling with my sissy."

"My name is Elena, and this is my husband, Bodhi. He's a doctor."

"I thought he was a boat inspector."

"Uh … he's a doctor when he's not inspecting boats."

"Well, I don't believe ya. I heard the both of ya kissin' in there." She snickered, her pale, freckled cheeks flushed.

Bodhi rolled his eyes. "Oh, jeez."

Elena tapped Josie's reddened nose and snickered. "You're a smart young lady, Josie. You caught us. We're not inspectors, and we *were* kissing."

Josie tittered. "I knew it."

Elena crossed her arms and grinned. "What's your room number? Maybe we can visit you and you can introduce us to your sissy."

"We're in room fifty-seven on C-deck." She licked her lollipop and offered them a bite.

Bodhi held up his hand and shook his head. "No thanks, kiddo. I'm trying to quit."

Elena nibbled the candy and winked. "Muy buena, Josie. It was our pleasure meeting you. Hasta luego ... which in Spanish means 'We will see you later.'"

Josie stifled a grin. "I can't wait to tell Sissy I caught you two kissin' in a lifeboat." She scurried away, blending into the growing crowd of sunbathers relaxing in lounge chairs lining the deck.

Bodhi and Elena stared at each other in silence, then burst into laughter. "Ay, Bodhi. The entire ship must know." She pointed toward the sunbathers. "They're staring at us."

Bodhi slid his hand over hers and tugged her in the opposite direction. "They're not staring. They're jealous ... Now, let me tell you about U-boats."

They interlocked fingers and strolled along the outer deck of the Lusitania, embracing the freedom they'd found in escaping the government agents and Phillip McMullin—even if it was short-lived.

A disturbance inside an empty breezeway soon interrupted the tranquil afternoon. A crewman shoved a woman into a corner and clutched her throat. Bodhi bull-rushed the man from behind, body-slamming him to the deck, while Elena pulled the woman to safety.

Bodhi hovered over the man and stabbed a threatening finger in his face. "Touch this woman again, and I'll break your jaw."

The man scrambled to his feet and escaped up a stairwell. Bodhi scooped up a leather journal from the deck, and knelt before the woman, resting his palm on her shoulder.

"Are you alright, ma'am?"

He presented the journal and asked, "Does this belong to you?"

The woman snatched it from his grip and held it to her breast as if cradling a child. She glanced up at him and whispered, "Thank you."

He gasped, taken aback by the glint of aquamarine in her stare. *The woman from the café,* he thought.

Elena patted her hand. "Are you traveling with anyone?"

The woman inhaled a quivering breath and shook her head slightly. "No. I was separated from my husband while traveling. I don't know how exactly, but—"

Bodhi intervened. "What's his name? Maybe we can help you find him."

She lowered her eyes and sighed. "I don't want to find him. I want to be free of him."

Bodhi and Elena glanced at each other, confused. Bodhi asked, "Can we escort you back to your cabin?"

Elena outstretched her arm, offering her hand. "I'm Elena, and this is my husband, Bodhi. He's a doctor. Are you hurt?"

She rose and gazed deep into his eyes, placing her palm on his cheek, running her fingers over a z-shaped scar on his temple, beneath his hairline. Her eyes misted, and her lower lip trembled.

She whispered, "Bodhi?"

She shook her head and lowered her eyes. "No. I can find my own way."

"Are you sure? What if this guy attacks you again?"

"He won't."

"Do you know him? Is he a crew member?"

"No. He was sent by my husband … Probably long gone by now."

Bodhi crinkled his brow, glanced toward the vast ocean, and back toward the woman. "Well, he couldn't have gone far."

"Trust me … he's gone."

She glanced at him as if she wanted to speak, but hesitated. The depth of her stare sent a chill up his spine. "I need to go. Thank you again." The woman gripped her journal and vanished down a wooden stairwell.

Elena squeezed his hand. "Who do you think she is, Cariño?"

"No idea. Hopefully, she's not a government spy or some anomaly of this timeline. And what's with the journal? It seemed like the guy was trying to steal it from her."

"My bones tingle with bad juju, Bodhi. We should leave this timeline."

"There's something curious about her, babe. I have to find out what it is first."

"You're not listening to me. We need to go. Something isn't right … and don't say I'm paranoid, or I'll slap you."

Bodhi chuckled. "I think we're both a little paranoid. We need to find out what's in that journal. I … need to find out what's in that journal."

"Vaya, Bodhi. How do you plan on doing that? The poor gringa has had enough trauma for one day."

"I don't know. Did you see the way she looked at me? She wanted to say something, but hesitated. This whole thing is creeping me out and driving me crazy at the same time."

"It'll have to wait. She said *adios* and disappeared."

"Well, she can't go far, obviously."

He shielded his eyes and gazed across miles of ocean. "We need to keep an eye out for the coast of Ireland. As long as we're surrounded by water, we're safe. Once we see the coast, we're out of here."

Bodhi and Elena continued their stroll around the great ship. The Lusitania embodied the richest of English society. A literal palace on the sea, and they couldn't help but be seduced by its nostalgic charm. Her fingers interlocked with his, tugging at him and guiding his arm around her shoulders. She snuggled into his body, causing their feet to stumble out of step. They chit-chatted for over an hour, hugging, kissing, and drinking up every precious moment together.

"I love you, Bodhi McMullin. If you want to see inside that woman's journal, I'll help you steal it."

Bodhi froze and squinted. "You just might get that chance."

Elena focused her attention on the direction of Bodhi's stare. Stretched out on a lounge chair beneath a plaid red and white blanket lay the woman, sound asleep, with the open journal on her lap, pen in hand.

Bodhi tiptoed next to her chair, careful not to disturb her. He peeked at the writing.

I've evaded Phillip all these years, but I'm petrified he will surely find me now that our son has arrived in this timeline. He has his spies everywhere. I can only hope ...

The deck beneath Bodhi's feet seemed to shudder. He collapsed onto the lounge chair next to the woman—Ethel—his long-lost mother. Knots curled his insides, pushing a sudden case of nausea into his throat. He glanced at Elena, his jaw hanging.

She whispered, "What is it, Cariño? Your face is as pale as leche."

The woman's eyes popped open; she gasped and slammed the journal shut. She tried to escape, but Bodhi grabbed her wrist.

"No. Please stay."

Ethel closed her eyes as if praying and lowered her head.

"I can't stay. I have to go. Please, let me go," she whimpered.

"Ethel? ... Mom? How can this be? Phillip has been searching for you for years. We didn't believe you were even alive."

"It's hard to find someone who doesn't want to be found."

"What do you mean? Gram sent you both away ... and somehow separated you. I'm sorry she did that to you, by the way."

She caressed his cheek. Her gaze touched his soul and unlocked years of long-forgotten emotions. "You shouldn't be, Bo Bo. Gram only did what I asked her to do."

"What do you mean? You wanted to leave?"

"It was the only way to save you from your father. Gram and I planned it for weeks."

"I don't understand what's happening …"

"I was broken, son. Manipulated by your father. I was more his prisoner than his wife … and he abused you. I couldn't protect you." She dabbed her tears. "The last time I took you to the hospital, I swore I'd never let him touch you again."

Elena slid next to Bodhi and rested her hand on his thigh.

"He controlled every second of my life, Bo. I was an addict and an alcoholic because of him, and he made sure I stayed that way."

"But you left *me* … when I needed you most. What kind of mother does that? All these years, and you never once thought about me? Never thought to come looking for me?"

Tears gushed from Ethel's cheeks. "Not a day went by that my heart didn't ache for you. I couldn't risk trying to find you, and I had no means to travel home. I knew Gram would raise you into a good man. And look at you … so strong, kind, and brave … and so handsome."

"No, you don't get to do that. Why did everyone lie to me? I deserved to know the truth. I spent years believing you and Dad were killed in an auto accident. Then Gram told me you opened a portal on a ski trip by chance and disappeared … Another lie."

"To protect you."

"To protect me? Or to stamp your one-way ticket to freedom?"

Elena patted his hand. "Bodhi, listen to what she's telling you. She was protecting you along with Gram. Don't you see? Gram separated them on purpose to help your mother escape and to save you."

Ethel sniffled. "I didn't want to give you up, if that's what you think. It was the hardest thing I've ever had to do, and I regret it every day. I've lived with this guilt for so long … and when I saw your face this morning,

I wanted to wrap my arms around you and never let go, and ... I wanted to tell you who I was and how much I've missed you, my precious Bo Bo."

"Why didn't you just leave him and take me with you?"

"I did—I tried so many times, and he always found us, Bo Bo. I didn't know what else to do, so I went to Gram and asked for her help. Two days before that, your father came home drunk. He flew into a jealous rage and beat me nearly unconscious. You were so little, but you tried to save me. He slapped you. Grabbed you. Flung you across the room into the wall. Your wrist was fractured, and your chin split open. Bruises were everywhere. I swore it would be the last time he'd ever touch you."

Ethel sobbed and reached for him. "I let go ... to break the cycle of abuse and save you from your father's cruelty. Breaking my own heart."

His heart pounded into his throat, unsure of what to feel. Anger? Resentment? Pity?

He rested his hands over hers, shocked at how fragile and vulnerable they felt. Skin like satin, knuckles swollen, trembling.

"Hold me, son. Please forgive me." She slouched and lowered her head—the shame of so many years weighing on her shoulders.

He sucked a deep breath and exhaled sharply, slowly resting his hands on her shoulders and raising her up. His hug was gentle and hesitant.

Ethel fell into him, sobbing, squeezing her frail arms around his waist, shoulders quivering as she wept years of heartbreak. Her salty tears moistened his shirt.

"I've missed you so much, my sweet, sweet boy."

Ethel handed him the journal.

"What is this, Mom?"

"The answers, Bodhi. Answers they tried to steal from me. And all the letters I wrote to you, but could never send. It was the only way I stayed sane and felt connected to you. I imagined what each of your birthdays looked like. Wondered what your hobbies were ... what your favorite food was … how tall you'd grown, how many times your heart got broken."

Bodhi glanced away, attempting to hide the tears streaking down his cheeks. He wiped his face with his sleeve and nodded. "I don't know if I can read them."

"You don't have to. I just wanted you to have them. To remember me … maybe someday understand my reasons and … forgive my desperation. Please keep my journal safe, son. You might find what you seek inside its pages."

The air crackled, and the snap of ozone filled his nostrils. Elena removed the Tempus Glass from her purse, its emerald sands agitated and glowing.

Her eyes widened. "Something's not right, Cariño. We have to go."

Ethel squeezed Bodhi's hands. Terror filled her eyes.

"He's found us … you're in danger. You must leave. Both of you."

Bodhi rose and turned to face the sound of heels tapping against the wooden deck behind him.

"Ah, looks like our family reunion is complete." Phillip clapped and grinned. "Thank you, son, for helping me find your mother."

EIGHT

Phillip kneeled next to Ethel and kissed the back of her hand like royalty, then stroked the crown of her head like an adored pet. "We are finally reunited, Sweetpea," he whispered.

"I'm here to rescue you … to take you far away so we can start our lives over. I've missed you … so much lost time to make up for … but I promise … I promise … I'll make it up to you." He cradled her in his arms while Ethel gazed at Bodhi, her chin resting on Phillip's shoulder, with an expression nearing hysteria.

Phillip released Ethel and straightened his hair, adjusting his denim collar. He turned towards Bodhi and grinned. "I have the compass. We can leave now, as we agreed. Once your mother and I reach our destination, I'll give it up as promised. All that mumbo-jumbo back at the facility was an act. I had to fool them into thinking I would help them get the timepiece and Tempus Glass."

Elena couldn't contain her disgust. "I don't believe you, bastardo. Why should we trust you? You're a viper and a liar."

Phillip snickered. "Still with the trust issues, huh, Elena? Best that we all decide where we stand. The Irish coast isn't far, and this ship has a date with the ocean floor. I don't like sinking ships."

"Of course you do," Elena snapped. "It's where you steal relics that do not belong to you and allow others to die to save your own skin. You're a coward ... a galley rat ready to jump ship."

Phillip grinned. "I know. Right? The irony of it all." He turned toward Bodhi and palmed his shoulder. "What do you say, son? Do you trust your old dad? Do we still have a deal?"

"No ... *Dad*. We don't." Bodhi handed Elena the journal and stood nose-to-nose with Phillip, prompting him to back up several steps.

Phillip raised a brow and clicked his tongue. "Always with the anger issues, boy. Should have enrolled you into anger counseling when you were a kid, I suppose."

"You weren't around, and I don't think I'm the one who needed a shrink."

"Well, I hope you've had enough time to catch up with your mom. *Because* ... it's time for her and me to journey to deeper waters. It's been real." He glanced at Ethel and extended his hand. Her silence was met with an impatient glare. "Ethel? Let's go."

Ethel rose and glanced at Bodhi before focusing her eyes on the deck. She crossed her arms and slowly shook her head. "I'm not going with you, Phillip." She raised her eyes to meet his.

"What do you mean, you're not going with me? Of course you are. Take my hand so we can get the hell out of here."

"No, Phillip. It's time you realized that I never loved you. I hated my life with you ... hated being your prisoner. It's the reason I escaped. I finally got away from you, Phillip, and it's taken this long for you to catch up to me. I'm not running anymore—so tired of running. I'm leaving with my son and his wife, and I want to spend whatever life I have left with them ... not you. It was *never* you. And I never want to see your face again. Not in this life or the next."

Phillip stepped toward her, raising the back of his hand, ready to strike. Bodhi shoved him backward and stabbed a meaty forefinger into his sternum. "Those days are over, buddy. You'll never lay a hand on her again. Or me."

Ethel locked arms with Bodhi and glared at Phillip. "Little boys grow up, and they remember. My son is a man, and you can't hurt him anymore, Phillip. You have no power over our lives. So go … go find whatever it is you seek because it won't be a life with me."

Phillip's face flushed, and his teeth gnashed. He stepped toward Ethel, fists clenched. Bodhi coldcocked him with a left hook that shuddered him to his knees. He rose, stammered backward, and wiped the blood from his busted lip, stunned.

His widened eyes darkened. Raising the compass like a wizard's talisman, he adjusted the dial, creating a thick fog that veiled the entire ship in a purplish haze.

Phillip sneered. "If you don't leave with me, Ethel, you'll die with your son on this ship."

"What are you talking about? What have you done?" Bodhi shouted.

"You and that chili pepper wife underestimated my power and knowledge. I've tethered all three of you to this ship. To die. You won't be capable of leaving its deck. Ever. Your new life begins at the bottom of the Atlantic … Actually, it ends."

As the Lusitania separated itself from Phillip's purple fog, a voice cried out from the top deck. "Torpedo coming! On the starboard side!"

Seconds later, the deck beneath them rumbled and pitched. Shockwaves knocked them to their hands and knees. A sharp explosion pierced his eardrums—the world muffled as if someone covered his head with a burlap sack. The noxious scent of burned coal filled the air like a thousand bad cigars. A cloud of blackened smoke billowed, blotting out the sun.

Phillip guffawed. "The clock is ticking. Come with me, Ethel, or you'll all die."

Bodhi lifted Elena and Ethel to their feet. Elena grasped his wrist. "We need to do something, Bodhi. We have to stop him, or this is where our story ends, Mi Amore. Let's put our brains together and make a plan."

Elena removed the Tempus Glass from her purse and pointed at the timepiece still clipped to his vest. "Are you ready?"

"Ready for what? We haven't put our brains together yet. What are you going to do?"

Elena chanted, stirring the dazzling green sands. All time and motion ceased.

Bodhi glanced at his surroundings. "You stopped time … Okay … that's good … now what?"

"Now we figure out what to do. I'm open to ideas, Bodhi. You spent the most time studying …"

"Me? I thought you had a plan."

"I'm thinking … help me think." She slapped his arm. "Ay ay ay."

Bodhi snapped his fingers and pointed at her. "A rift. We need to create a rift in space and time to escape."

"Do whatever you're going to do, Bodhi … before time restarts. Pronto!"

"Okay … okay. Hold my hand … Ethel, you too. We gotta make this work."

A depression in space, like a distorted sound wave, opened a vortex in front of them with an otherworldly thrum.

"There it is. Let's go!" Bodhi shouted.

"Wait. What about Josie and her sister?" Elena pleaded.

"Are you kidding right now? They die … or they survive. We don't know. They're part of the history of this ship. We don't have time to save them."

"Their mama is waiting for them in Liverpool, Bodhi. We have to save them," she cried. "C-deck. Room fifty-seven. I'll be right back. Do nothing until I get back." She darted along the outer deck and disappeared down a stairwell.

"Elena! What the hell, man? Have you lost your mind?" He threw up his arms. "Ah, shit."

Ethel squeezed his hand. "Maybe they survive, son. Maybe this is *how* they survive. Trust her. She's brave and smart. You did well in choosing her."

"That's not helping. The vortex is already unstable. She better hurry, or there'll be three more unidentified victims of the Lusitania for the history books."

Elena returned with Josie and her sister, both wearing life vests.

Bodhi jerked his head backward. "How in the hell did you manage that?"

"I have skills, too. No time to explain. Help me with the lifeboat."

Josie gripped her older sister's hand and gazed up at Bodhi, awestruck—her eyes as wide as cue balls and her jaw hanging open.

"How are ya doing this? Are the two of ya angels from Heaven?"

Bodhi scooped her into his arms. "Something like that. Come on … get in the boat, girls."

As the lifeboat lowered with its two skittish occupants, Bodhi leaned over the rail and shouted, "Get as far away from the ship as you can. Someone will pick you up in a few hours. Understand? Everything will be alright."

The girls huddled together as the craft gently entered the water.

"Bodhi! Hurry! The vortex is wobbling. It's not going to hold."

His heart sank at the sudden realization that someone had to keep Phillip from entering the rift.

"One of us is going to have to stay behind. We can't allow Phillip to follow." Bodhi lowered his head. "You both go. I'll stay."

"No!" Elena shrieked.

Ethel took Bodhi by the hands. "You go, son. I'll keep Phillip distracted." She shrugged and smiled. "It's my job, Bo Bo … it's always been my job…"

"You don't have to do this. I'll catch up," he insisted.

"Yes, I do. Go live your life. Remember me … maybe find it in your heart to forgive me." Her tears gushed as she nibbled on her trembling lower lip.

"Goddammit." Bodhi's heart pounded … emotional walls deep within his psyche crumbled, and childhood memories of his mother flooded his mind like a collage. Not the drug addict or the alcoholic accused of neglect and abuse. But the mother who nurtured and protected him—the one who sacrificed everything to keep him safe and give him a fighting chance at a happy life. He remembered now … he remembered everything.

"There's nothing to forgive. I know you did the best you could."

Elena screamed, "Bodhi! We have to go. It's closing. Vámonos!"

Bodhi hugged Ethel, leaving a gentle kiss on her forehead. "Goodbye, Mom. I love you. I've always loved you … Along the way, I … I simply forgot. But I remember. I understand why you made the decisions you did." He stifled the clump of sobs rising in his throat as he wiped the wetness from her cheeks. Time resumed, and chaos ensued.

Bodhi released his hug, grabbed Elena's hand, and jumped into the portal's deteriorating jaws. They vanished seconds before the vortex fizzled.

NINE

The gentle crash of waves against the shoreline prompted Bodhi to open his eyes. Elena interlocked her fingers inside his and locked eyes with him. Her brows rose to a peak, and she tilted her head.

"I'm so sorry, Mi Amore. Just when you found your mother, you—"

"It's okay." He raised Ethel's journal and forced a half-hearted smile.

Elena caressed his cheek. "Your mother proved her love for you. She sacrificed herself to save us. No matter how she failed you in the past, she redeemed herself with such a loving act. That's how a mother loves her child, Bodhi. It should bring you peace."

Bodhi stiffened his lips and inhaled sharply. He nodded and whispered, "It does."

"We can't stay here, Bodhi. Gram's beach house is the first place they'll look for us."

"I know. I have a condo in Burbank that Phillip knows nothing about. We can buy some time there until we figure out our next move."

Bodhi slipped through the screen door, allowing it to slam behind him, then reemerged with two helmets in hand. He tossed her the smaller of the two and grinned.

"Oh no … no, no, no. I'm not riding that beastly machine with you. I'll walk first."

"Come on, babe. I'll take it easy … slow curves and as many breaks as you need."

"Por Dios, Bodhi. I don't trust you. You get these crazy, loco eyes when you ride that thing. I know why Cassie's mother forbade you to ride with her."

"Alright, alright. We'll take the SUV. What happened to the wild-spirited woman I married? You used to be fearless." He chuckled as he grabbed a stack of letters and parcels from the mailbox and tossed them on the seat between them.

"Fearless, Bodhi. Not estúpida. Take me somewhere to eat. I'm starving," she huffed as she crossed her arms and stared out the window.

"Yes, my queen. I know just the place before we leave town. It's a bit spicy. Can you handle it?"

Her lips widened, erasing the scowl. She shook her head. "Venga, gringo. The real question is, can you?"

They rolled into Bodhi's garage in Burbank as the sun faded. He fumbled with his keys and swung the door wide, bracing it with his foot until she entered.

"Ay caramba, Bodhi. What's that smell? A dead carcass? Fúchila."

"Oh, man. Somebody didn't empty the trash." He gagged as he yanked the tie-string on the plastic bag and tossed it down the trash chute outside the door.

"I think that 'somebody' was you … The lights don't work either, Señor."

"Not sure when we paid the electricity last."

Sparks ignited, and a tinge of sulfur filled the air. He lit several of Cassie's old candles around the condo, casting a flickering, golden glow across the walls. Soft, warm candlelight bathed Elena's face, highlighting the rigid contours of her jawline. A tiny flame reflected in her darkened eyes, gazing back at him, raising his pulse.

She plopped on the sofa and patted the cushion next to her. "Sit with me, Corazón. Hold me in your arms. I'm so freezing," she said as she crossed her arms and pretended to shiver.

"Yeah, I can see how cold you are," he snickered. Bodhi lifted a fuzzy blanket from the back of the sofa, draped it over her lap, and collapsed beside her. She snuggled into his hug and sighed, caressing his cheek. "Gracias, Mi Corazón."

"For what?"

"For not making me ride that awful Harley beast."

"Don't mention it."

"What are we going to do, Bodhi?"

He heaved a breath and raised his brows. "Well, right now, we're going to relax. Tomorrow, we'll figure this out."

Elena closed her eyes and rested her head on his shoulder. "I just want to fall asleep in your arms. I can't keep my eyes open no more."

"That makes two of us."

"Sweet dreams, *Bo Bo*," she giggled.

"Ah, jeez. Don't call me that. Please."

The rhythm of her soft breaths caused his head to bob, lulling him into a peaceful slumber.

Bodhi rose as sunlight poured through the slits in the living room blinds. Elena softly snored, snuggled in the corner of the sofa, barely visible inside her mountain of blankets. It was quiet. The ticks of a clock and a random chirp outside their window were the only sounds.

Bodhi opened Ethel's journal and ran his fingers over the pages. Her cursive was difficult to read, so he used a magnifying glass he found in a kitchen drawer to help decipher her scribbles.

My Dear Son,

I can never express how the ache in my heart torments me every waking moment. I never wanted to leave you. It was the hardest thing I've ever had to do. Harder than recovering from addiction, harder than enduring the abuse and punishment from years of living with your father. Bruises heal. Drugs and alcohol eventually leave the bloodstream. But a fracture in a mother's heart from the loss of a child never mends. The betrayal in your innocent eyes and your warbling cries were a dagger to my soul, and every night when I close my eyes, I relive the horror. But if ripping my heart out meant keeping you safe from your father's beatings, it was worth it. Please don't judge me harshly. I saw no other way out. My life has been lonely without you, but quiet and peaceful without your father. I've been free from his terror, but never free from my brokenness. My only wish is…

A loose page tucked into the journal's cover slipped onto his lap. The yellowed page appeared fragile, like an old scroll written in a foreign language.

Bodhi smoothed the page across the top of his coffee table and scanned it with his cell phone flashlight. Elena stirred, arching her back and stretching her right fist toward the ceiling. She yawned, blinked, and asked, "¿Qué pasa? What are you doing?"

"I found this letter inside my mother's journal. Maybe this is why Phillip's thug was trying to steal it from her. Ethel wasn't giving me the journal, Elena. She was giving me the letter … the '*answers.*'"

She tossed the blankets and scooched to the sofa's edge like a curious teenager. "Madre de Dios … That's written in Latin." She closed her eyes and made the sign of the Cross.

"I agree. Three years of Latin, and I can barely make out a single word. We'll need a translator."

Elena wrinkled her brow. "I was raised Catholic. Latin was one of the languages my parents forced me to learn. I speak three languages, you know. You don't need an interpreter. I can tell you what it says."

"You never cease to impress me, Elena. How did I not know that?"

She shrugged. "You never asked. There are many things you don't know about me, Señor Bo Bo."

He rolled his eyes, turned the scroll towards her, and jerked open the blinds. Elena ran her forefinger over the text and mumbled.

Bodhi couldn't contain his impatience. "What? What does it say?"

She raised her palm, focusing on the writing. "Cállate, hombre. Let me concentrate."

Elena waved an impatient hand. "Get me some paper … and a pen."

Bodhi tossed a yellow notepad and a stubby pencil onto the coffee table and crossed his arms, squinting. Elena scribbled several lines.

"Some of these words make no sense. I've never seen them before."

"I thought you could read Latin."

Her eyes narrowed, shooting darts at his. She scoffed. "I can. But some of these words, I don't recognize."

"Then maybe we should find an expert in Latin."

"Give me a minute to think. Huy, Bodhi, you're making my brain hurt." She wagged a scolding finger. "Sit down. Over there. Find something else to do before your eyes light this paper on fire."

Bodhi flopped into his easy chair, his left ankle resting on his right knee, and his fingers interlocked behind his head. He softly whistled and watched as she worked.

Elena glared at him, raising an eyebrow, and continued scribbling.

"Sorry," he mumbled, leaning forward and planting his elbows on his knees.

"Bodhi, if I'm reading this right, there is an ancient tome written by an angel named Cassiel buried in a bunker of secret archives at the Vatican. It names Cassiel as the Guardian of Time, and he alone can reclaim what is lost … referring to the relics, I believe."

"So, what does all of that mean?"

"It means we need to find this tome and read it."

Elena glared at him, nibbling on her lower lip.

He raised his palms and shrugged. "What?"

"Bodhi, there's a warning here."

"What kind of warning?"

"It says, 'He who holds the Trinity holds the fate of time itself. To return the relics is to surrender what was never meant to be held.' It goes on to say that the relics are immortal and cannot be destroyed. They must be returned to Cassiel."

"Okay, so we return them to Cassiel. How do we do that?"

"It doesn't say. That's why we must go to Rome … to the Vatican, and find out. We need the tome, but we'll need to break into the Vatican's secret vault." She grimaced. "How do we do that?"

"Maybe we ask," he casually replied.

"Ask?" she scoffed, rolling her eyes. "Why didn't I think of that?"

"Hey, it's my understanding that scholars can request to view certain documents, codices, artifacts, etc., from the Vatican archives for research purposes. I'll need to convince somebody that I qualify. I have a doctorate in medicine, after all."

"Bodhi, there's another warning here." Her brows formed a peak as she nibbled her thumbnail.

"From the look on your face, I'm afraid to ask."

"It says the one who returns the Trinity to the angel Cassiel is doomed to the same fate as the angel."

"And … what fate is that?"

"To be cut off from the world and everything in it … *everyone* in it. Oh, Bodhi, maybe there's another way. Maybe we can hide the relics and prevent them from ever being found. Or give them to the Vatican."

"They'll never stop hunting us. As long as they possess the compass, there's nowhere to hide."

"We have to know what's in that tome," she muttered.

Bodhi plopped next to her and wrapped his arm around her shoulders. "Start packing. We need to book a flight to Rome. And hey, I've never seen the Vatican, have you?"

"Me neither … Aw, to go to Rome, Bodhi…" Her eyes fluttered like a little girl in a doll store.

"My mama dreamed of taking me to Rome and Vatican City."

"Your mama can thank me later. I've got my passport, but we need to get yours. I know someone who can help expedite that, then we'll check for flights.

TEN

Elena dragged him toward Saint Peter's Square like a giddy teenager, eyes wide and lips slightly parted. A sobering awe washed over Bodhi, sensing the energy of so much history radiating from the stone square.

"I must be dreaming, Mi Amore." Elena lowered her head, crossed herself, and mumbled, "Protégenos, Santísima Madre."

Bodhi locked eyes with her and touched her chin. "Are you crying?"

She glanced away, wiped her cheeks, and sniffled. "No. Why? ... Maybe I am. So, what..."

"So, stay focused. We're not tourists, babe. We're here on a mission. This isn't like you to get all misty-eyed on a mission and—"

"I'm sorry. It's so overwhelming to my heart. I keep thinking about my mama and—"

He rested his hands on her shoulders. "There'll be time for that later, sweetheart. Right now, I need my badass woman to have my back."

She pursed her lips, wiped her cheeks again, and nodded. "Okay ... Okay. I'm fine. Vámonos."

The vast, open space seemed endless, framed by Bernini's magnificent colonnades, which swept out like welcoming arms, embracing visitors from every corner of the earth. Bernini's masterpiece—designed to embrace the faithful—now seemed more like a fortress, its columns standing sentry, keeping watch over the Vatican's ancient mysteries.

His pulse quickened as they moved deeper into the square. Before them, the Basilica loomed, majestic and ominous, its façade glowing gold under the early afternoon light. Statues of saints lined the rooftop, their stony eyes fixed on the heavens, faces carved in expressions of divine serenity. He sensed the weight of their stare, their silent vigil laden with judgment—or a warning.

In the center of the square, an Egyptian obelisk rose defiantly toward the sky, a pagan relic stolen from Heliopolis, its presence a riddle in itself. It cast a long shadow across the cobblestones, pointing like an accusatory finger toward the Vatican's heart. "An axis mundi," he muttered, recalling its symbolism—a bridge between earth and heaven, man and God. Or perhaps, in this place of power, between the mortal and divine secrets that lay beneath their feet.

Tourists bumped into them, moving like shadows, faces turned upward, unaware of the timeless mysteries that lurked beneath the cobblestone. They snapped photos, oblivious to the riddles hidden in plain sight, encrypted within the architecture itself. His eyes traced the path from the obelisk to the Basilica's dome, the grand design forming a perfect line—an ancient alignment meant to harness celestial power.

"Bodhi, why is there an Egyptian obelisk in the center of the square?"

"It's a symbol … like everything around us. It's a statement of Christianity's triumph over paganism." He pointed. "See what's engraved on its side?"

"*Christus vincit, Christus regnat, Christus imperat* … Christ conquers, Christ reigns, Christ rules," she replied in a semi-dreamy state.

"Exactly. The message is embedded in every stone around us. It's the *Vatican*, sweetheart. We made it. I promise, your mama is smiling from heaven."

He glanced over his shoulder, tensing from the weight of unseen eyes. The saints above stood motionless, yet he swore one shifted slightly, its suspicious gaze now fixed on them.

They ambled toward the Basilica's steps, the ancient cobblestones echoing their footsteps. Each step brought them closer to the truth—and to the dangers that guarded it. Saint Peter's Square wasn't just a place of worship; it was a labyrinth of symbols, a puzzle constructed by those who knew the power of secrets. Bodhi and Elena were about to walk straight into its cryptic heart.

Days earlier, Elena spoke to the secretary of the Archivist and Librarian for the Holy Roman Catholic Church to inquire about Bodhi's request to access the Vatican's secret archive. Request denied. Even if accepted, it would take months to gain access, time they didn't have. Plan B was their only option.

They exited Saint Peter's Square and approached the Porta di Santa Anna. Bodhi's pulse quickened as the ancient archway emerged from the murky shadows. Elena scurried behind him, keeping pace. Tucked inconspicuously at the edge of Vatican City, Swiss soldiers guarded the entrance in vibrant crimson, gold, and blue uniforms—living relics sworn to protect the Pope and the secrets within these sacred walls. Their halberds gleamed beneath the pale Vatican sun, a ceremonial display concealing centuries of discipline and lethal precision.

The arched gateway was deceptively ordinary, its stone facade blending seamlessly with the surrounding architecture. More than a passage; it was a threshold—a portal into the hidden nucleus of the Vatican, a place where knowledge is power and history is guarded with zealous secrecy.

Bodhi's eyes traced the Latin inscription etched below the arch—words worn by time yet still commanding reverence: *Custodiunt Mysteria— They Guard the Mysteries.*

Beyond the gate, a cobbled pathway disappeared into obscurity, curving sharply out of sight. It led to the Cortile del Belvedere, a courtyard that seemed innocuous to the untrained eye but was meticulously designed to disorient intruders. To the right, a narrow corridor flanked by centuries-old frescoes concealed the entrance to a staircase descending into the earth—toward the Vatican's most forbidden repository.

Archivum Secretum Vaticanum—The Secret Archives. A place spoken of in hushed whispers by historians and conspiracy theorists alike. A labyrinth of ancient documents, forbidden texts, and artifacts shrouded in myth. Here, among the dust of ages, lay the records of inquisitions, lost gospels, and correspondences that could rewrite history—or destroy it. The Tome of Cassiel would be amongst these records, about to give up its ancient secrets the moment Bodhi and Elena deciphered its pages.

Bodhi's gaze flicked to a security camera, its black lens unblinking, tracking their every movement. The Vatican's defenses were as advanced as they were ancient—a blend of technology and tradition, ensuring the knowledge within remained untouched by the outside world.

He stepped forward, feeling the burden of centuries pressing down on his shoulders. A Swiss guard moved to intercept them, his expression stoic, eyes cold and calculating. Elena, using Bodhi as a shield, removed the Tempus Glass and silently chanted as Bodhi attempted to stall the guard's inquiries. The emerald sands stirred, and time froze.

Bodhi hesitated, glancing once more at the cherubs' carved faces. Their stony smiles almost dared him to step further inside. Taking a deep breath, he snatched the guard's keys and ID badge and crossed the threshold, Elena a step behind. They made it inside the Vatican's most sacred and dangerous vault. A vast library containing the history of the world lay before them. Miles of metallic shelves housing tens of thousands of ancient books, codices, tomes, maps, and documents unseen and untouched for centuries.

Ethel's scroll directed them toward a hidden corner rumored to secure history's rarest and most dangerous relics. Relics like the Chronovisor, a device believed to allow the viewing of historical events through a technology that captured images from the past using electromagnetic waves. And the Grand Grimoire, a tome so evil it's kept under lock and key and forbidden to be accessed by anyone but the Pope. The Tome of Cassiel was said to reside inside this grotto, concealing the secrets of time travel from prying eyes.

Bodhi and Elena moved swiftly through the endless aisles of metal shelves that stretched from floor to ceiling, lined with a vast collection of deteriorating books dusted by centuries, some locked away behind wire cages for their unspeakable sins.

The air cooled as they dashed along the dim aisles, filled with the blended scents of decaying paper, damp stone, and mildew like an old basement. A map inked on the scroll led to an eerie hallway down a flight of steps etched into the stone.

A chill overtook them as they descended the staircase, the echoes of their footsteps swallowed by the oppressive silence. The passage narrowed, and ancient walls pressed inward as if conspiring to keep intruders away. A dim blue light illuminated the passage, radiating from soft lighting embedded in the upper walls. At the end of the corridor, they faced a reinforced door—a monolithic slab of steel embedded within the rock like a fortress gate. It bore no markings, no visible handle—only a single security panel glowing faintly with an unnatural orange light. This was the entrance to the most guarded area of the Vatican's secret archive, a place few knew existed and even fewer had ever seen.

The orange glow of the security panel beamed steadily as he passed the guard's ID over the sensor. No effect.

"Damnit. It's not working," he whispered.

"Bodhi, time is suspended. Maybe the function of the lock is also suspended. We should restart time and try again."

He nodded, flashing a crooked smile. "That's why I bring you along on these adventures. We need to work fast." He pointed at the ceiling. "Those are cameras."

"Ay, I know. Here goes."

As time resumed, the orange light pulsated in rhythm with a low, steady thrum. Bodhi slid the ID card over the sensor, breathing a sigh of relief as the lock clicked and the door rolled across a metal track in the floor, disappearing into a slot in the stone wall. Beyond the door was a locked cage similar to the ones they passed in the aisles. He fumbled with the keys until he located the one that opened the crypt.

"Hurry, Bodhi."

They scanned shelves of ancient tomes, rolled scrolls, artifacts, and binders of yellowed documents—some only fragments. Above them, red lights swirled in eerie silence.

"They're onto us, babe. Where the hell is it?"

Red lasers filled the cage like a light show in Vegas. Four soldiers focused their rifles on Bodhi's chest. One guard barked an order.

Bodhi glanced at Elena. "You speak German?" She shook her head. "No. What do we do?"

The guard shouted again, gesturing with his rifle for them to kneel.

Bodhi kicked the cage door shut, jamming the key into the lock and breaking it off.

He craned his neck toward Elena. "Find the book and get us the hell out of here!"

The soldiers banged on the cage door, attempting to unlock it before realizing what Bodhi had done. Cursing in German, one soldier struck the lock with the butt of his rifle over and over. Bodhi did his best to stall them.

"Hurry, babe! These guys are pissed. I don't know how much longer the lock can hold."

"I'm hurrying as fast as I can!"

"Well, hurry faster..."

Elena lifted a weathered tome from the center of a shelf, tucked between two leather-bound codices. A warded lock secured its gold-plated binding—the raised image of an angel with a triangle in his right hand and three orbs at his feet decorated the cover.

"I think I found it!"

Bodhi turned, snatched the tome, and examined it. "No way. Hit the gas pedal, girlfriend! Get us the hell out of here!"

The orange flame of a blowtorch sent cherry sparks flying, bouncing off the cage and onto the ground like fireworks. The soldiers flung the door wide and rushed inside.

Elena chanted, stimulating the sands of the Tempus Glass into action. A violent vortex roared into existence, filling the crypt with colorful, blinding lights and sending the guards fleeing for their lives. They didn't hesitate to dive into its mouth. Moments later, they found themselves in the middle of Saint Peter's Square. Bodhi's eyes widened. "We needed to get farther away than this, Elena."

"This was the best I could do."

"Okay, okay ... let's pump the brakes and think for a second."

In the distance, the shrill of sirens approached.

"We don't *have* a second, Bodhi."

He removed the timepiece and hummed, hugging Elena and the Tome.

"No, not here," she shouted.

"Why?"

"Are you joking right now?"

"No, no. You're right. It'll create a shitstorm of media attention."

Bodhi waved his arms frantically to hail a cabbie.

"The Grand Hotel Palace, please."

The driver's face was contorted and confused. He shrugged. Elena pushed Bodhi aside and hollered in Italian, "Take us to the Grand Hotel Palace!"

They sped away into congested traffic, away from the sirens and chaos. Elena sighed and rested her head on his shoulder. Bodhi patted her thigh and gripped Cassiel's Tome beneath his jacket. The heist was complete, and the getaway was underway. But Vatican cameras captured their faces and have probably already identified them.

The cabbie's tires bounced off the curb in front of the Grand Hotel Palace. Bodhi stuffed a wad of cash into the driver's hand and followed Elena to the sidewalk. "Grazie."

As they strolled toward the entrance, Bodhi stopped, locked arms with Elena, and reversed direction.

"What are you doing? The hotel is the other way."

"Those are detectives loitering at the entrance."

ELEVEN

They scurried along the cobblestone, taking a sharp left down Via Liguria, huddling between rows of shrubs and a cream-colored concrete wall.

"We need to run, Bodhi. We'll never make it on the plane."

"We wouldn't make it past security, babe." He flashed the golden Tome. "This thing would set off every metal detector in the airport."

Elena pointed upward. "I think we need a safer place to hide."

Bodhi traced the path of her finger to the cameras protruding from the salmon-colored balconies above them.

"Damn. Maybe a park? Let me check *maps* on my phone."

He expanded the screen with his fingertips and nodded. "Ah-ha. There's a good-sized park less than a quarter of a mile from here." He inhaled sharply and pointed. "That way … Let's roll."

Bodhi rested his hands on his knees, gasping for breath. He stood, using the front of his T-shirt to wipe his reddened face, exposing his dad's gut. "Whew. I gotta spend more time in the gym when we get home."

Elena patted his belly and smirked. "Maybe no more tamales for you, Gordo."

"That too. I think I've gained twenty pounds. You gotta stop cooking so much. Don't get me wrong, your cooking is killer, but it's *literally* killing me."

"Nobody force-feeds you. I make plenty of food for leftovers. It's not my fault your mouth wants to eat everything your eyes see."

He chuckled. "How do you stay so fit and trim, Latina Barbie?"

"By not eating all the leftovers. You make it easy."

"Ah."

Elena removed the Tempus Glass and planted herself on a wooden park bench beneath the shade of an umbrella pine tree. "Focus, Bodhi. We should go."

Over a dozen secret service agents converged on them like a wolf pack, pointing weapons and shouting orders in Italian, "Get on the ground … hands behind your head!".

Elena glanced at Bodhi. "They want us on the ground."

The agents confiscated the relics, the tome, and their passports. Cold, metallic cuffs constricted the blood in his wrists. Two agents lifted him by the armpits and stuffed him into the back of a black SUV. He could only watch as they forced Elena into a separate SUV and sped away, lights flashing.

Elena and Bodhi rested on a lumpy, slate-gray, office-style loveseat in a ten-by-ten room. Neon lights illuminated the rose-colored plaster walls and stained gray carpet. The only other objects in the room were two stainless steel chairs and a fake houseplant in the corner next to a glass end table. The air reeked of cigarette ash and mildew. Before them was a windowless wooden door. The rumble of a furnace kicked on, creating a flow of stale, warm air.

She interlocked her fingers with his and whispered, "What will they do with us?"

The door creaked open. Agent Abara entered, followed by a woman dressed in a navy pantsuit, heels, and auburn hair pulled into a tight bun. She lugged a compact laptop and a manila folder.

Bodhi glanced at Elena and raised a brow. "I think we're about to find out."

Abara grinned and gestured towards his partner. "Surprised to see me? Allow me to introduce Agent Samantha Hughes. She'll be taking notes and assisting with today's briefing."

Samantha flashed a nervous, gentle smile. "Sam. Call me, Sam."

Bodhi scowled. "What is this, Abara? You have what you want. How 'bout you let us go and call it even, huh?"

Abara cocked his head and folded his arms. "If that is your wish, we can make that arrangement, Doctor. But first, please listen to our proposal."

Elena sneered. "Your proposals do not interest us. The chalado games you play are dangerous, Señor Abara."

Abara clicked his tongue and continued. "I'll come straight to the point and not waste your time or mine. We want to recruit you. To assist with our studies of the relics. We want you both to lead our team."

Bodhi scoffed and pointed toward Elena. "What *she* said."

Abara leaned forward and steepled his fingers across his lips. "Doctor ... Elena. Our team of scientists and experts is already hard at work studying the powers of the artifacts and quickly deciphering the tome you discovered in the Vatican's archives. Your input would be invaluable to our research. Please reconsider. You've proven yourselves as clever and formidable."

Samantha opened her laptop, balancing it on her thighs. She slid a pair of black-rimmed smart-glasses across the bridge of her nose and glanced at Abara, awaiting his response. He nodded and pointed to her device.

Samantha flipped open the manila folder and shuffled through several documents. "Your connections to the artifacts are vital to our research. Your experience with time travel could have a profound impact on the direction of our research and the safety of our team."

She focused her stare on Bodhi. "Your father has been a tremendous help, but as I'm sure you realize, he's unstable. Unreliable."

Bodhi guffawed. "You just now figured that out? I'm sorry, but we're not interested in working with you, my father, or anyone. We choose to live out our lives in peace before you two destroy everything. You have no idea what you're dealing with, do you? Not to sound trite, but this is a literal Pandora's Box … a quandary of unimaginable danger you're about to unleash on the world. Ya sure you wanna do that?"

Samantha removed her smart glasses, nibbling on the earpiece. She narrowed her eyes. "Then help us, Doctor. You took an oath to save people, didn't you? Your voices will be heard and respected. You'll have as much say in decision-making as anyone on our team, answering only to Agent Abara and me."

Bodhi rolled his eyes. "Gee, that all sounds peachy. I took a *medical* oath to help people with their *medical* conditions. These relics must be returned to their source to protect mankind from an apocalyptic disaster. That's all that needs to happen here. You have the relics and an instruction manual. Good luck. Can we go now, before you blow up the universe? We have a couple of items on our bucket list we'd like to check off before that happens, if you don't mind."

Abara tapped on his cell phone and mumbled, "Send her in."

A female agent pushed the door open and escorted Cassie inside.

"Daddy?" She wore the same powder-blue UCLA hoodie and jeans from the last time he saw her. His heart sank. Her eyes were wide with confusion as she shuffled across the floor and wedged between Bodhi and Elena like a child crawling into her parents' bed.

Abara folded his arms and leaned back in his seat as if palming a royal straight flush. His eyes darkened, and his ivory smile beamed. "I apologize for the unexpected family reunion, Doctor. We have your daughter, her husband, and your grandson in custody for their own protection. We've taken great care of them, I assure you."

"What games are you people playing here? This is bullshit. What do they have to do with this?"

"Everything. Like you, Cassie possesses the gift of time travel. She's agreed to cooperate and join our team."

Bodhi furrowed his brow and glared at Cassie. She shrugged and lowered her eyes.

"They threatened to take away Little William, Dad. I had no choice."

Bodhi stood and raised a fist. "What the hell are you doing, Abara? Don't play games with my family. You *have* what you need. My daughter has nothing to do with this. Let her go."

"If you and Elena agree to take her spot on our team, she and her family will be free to leave. Deal?"

Bodhi glanced at Elena, then glared at Abara. "Deal. Now let her go."

Abara rose and extended his hand toward Bodhi. "Excellent. I'll leave you and Elena in Sam's capable hands and escort Ms. Cassie back to her family and arrange their journey home ... wherever home may be."

The flight from Rome was long and turbulent. He hadn't slept well, and Elena's restlessness only added to his uneasiness. Teasing her for mumbling in her sleep and using him as a pillow, the entire flight only sparked her ire instead of her usual playfulness. They ate breakfast on the private jet and spent the last hour and fifteen minutes in the back of a black sedan traveling to an unknown destination. The dense trees surrounding them could exist in any forest in the world. He couldn't shake the look on Cassie's face as Abara took her away, rubbing the back of his neck and pinching the bridge of his nose. Warmth from Elena's grasp on his wrist pulled him from his thoughts and directed his eyes toward hers.

She whispered, "Stay alert and focused, Mi Amore."

Agent Hughes directed them toward an elevator that transported them hundreds of feet below the Earth's surface. They followed Agent Hughes down a long, dimly lit hallway into an empty amphitheater. In the center was a round eight-foot stage. Three four-foot-tall stainless-steel pillars formed a triangle in the middle of the stage, each supporting one relic. A pulsating emerald beam connected the relics. Crimson curtains covering the amphitheater walls absorbed a low thrum emanating from the triangle.

Bodhi glanced at Elena, then glared at Agent Hughes. "Well, that's a disturbing sight. You didn't waste any time setting up shop, did ya?"

"We followed the instructions within the tome to the letter, Doctor. You'll find we are quite thorough in our approach to the safety of our team … which includes both of you."

"And what are we doing today, Agent Hughes? What's your grand plan?"

"The stage is set … quite literally," she snickered, "for you, Elena, and Phillip to complete your first task."

"Phillip? Why Phillip? You said yourself he's unreliable."

"True, but he's experienced with the Mariner's Compass, and the most knowledgeable of the relic."

Bodhi frowned and shrugged. "So, *he* claims. How do you know that? Have you searched for an alternate?"

"We have. A young lady showed promise and assisted us recently, but we lost her."

"Lost her? How'd you manage that?"

Agent Hughes lowered her eyes, avoiding his glare, and softly replied, "We're not sure."

Elena crossed her arms and huffed. "That's comforting."

"We've recruited another, but more testing needs to happen before she's ready to contribute and—"

A familiar voice echoed behind them. "My favorite son and daughter-in-law. You kids ready for some fun? Hope ya packed light, cuz we're about to change the world."

The back of Bodhi's neck prickled. He scowled and turned toward Agent Hughes. "This is the best you've got? You want to put the fate of the universe into the hands of Larry the Cable Guy?"

"Ah, now that hurts, son. Already pitching a little hissy fit, I see."

Bodhi snatched Phillip by the throat and pushed a fist into his face. Elena wrapped her arm around Bodhi's and tugged him toward her. "Not here, Cariño. He isn't worth it."

Agent Hughes stepped between them and raised a calming hand. "Gentlemen, please take your seats. We have a lot to cover before your first mission, and we'll require everyone's full cooperation if we're going to be successful."

Phillip raised his palms and shrugged. "You heard the lady. Take your seats. We're gonna be busier than a one-legged cat in a sandbox."

Bodhi shook his head and threw up his arms. "I can't do this, Agent. The man's breath is ninety-proof. How the hell is he going to manage his duties? I'm not risking the safety of my wife on a mission with the town drunk."

Agent Hughes planted herself in a seat, crossed her legs, and pinched the bridge of her nose. "Doctor McMullin, it's crucial to the mission that we don't delay. I understand your concerns. I had no idea he was going to show up inebriated—"

"Inebriated? I had a couple of cool ones. To steady my nerves. I'm ready. I was born for this. Now, how about less chit-chat and more action?"

Hughes ignored him and twisted her body toward Bodhi and Elena. "We have another option, Doctor. We've tested the Mariner's Compass with another subject."

Bodhi's eyes widened. "Well, there you go. Let's bench *Shakes the Clown* here and replace him with the rookie."

She bit her lip and hesitated. "You're not going to like it."

He crossed his arms and raised a discerning brow. "What do you mean?"

She heaved a breath and sighed. "It's Cassie … your daughter."

"No, absolutely not. Abara promised he'd take her home."

"She hasn't left yet, and those are your options, Doctor. I need a decision…"

"You wanna bench me?" Phillip shouted. "That girl's barely out of diapers. This is bullshit. What are we waiting for? Ya'll are making my ass burn."

Bodhi stood and paced around the stage. The last thing he wanted to see happen was for Cassie to be pulled into their mess. But Phillip is as drunk as a turd and there's no way he's going to trust him with Elena's life or his own.

He pointed at Phillip. "Get your ass out of here and sleep it off, Phil," then craned his neck toward Hughes and nodded. "Get Cassie."

Hughes raised her smartwatch to her lips. "Bring McMullin's daughter and send someone in to pick up Phillip."

Phillip stood defiantly, crossing his arms and stomping his foot. "Well, I ain't leaving. We had a deal, Hughes—finish the tasks, and send me back to Ethel."

Agent Hughes narrowed the distance between herself and Phillip and squinted. "You *are* leaving. Otherwise, you won't be returning to your wife."

Bodhi's eyes lit up. "His wife? Where is she? Where's Ethel?"

Hughes stepped toward Bodhi, her heels tapping on the floor. "She didn't make it off the Lusitania. Not before it sank. I'm very sorry."

The lump in his throat turned to rage in his heart. Bodhi tackled Phillip to the ground, pounding his face into unconsciousness. "You son of a bitch!"

Two men in jumpsuits lifted Bodhi by the armpits off Phillip and dragged him to the other side of the room. Two others removed Phillip's limp body from the amphitheater.

"Calm down, bud. I don't want to taser you," a guard warned.

Bodhi heaved a ragged breath and relaxed. He rose and exposed his hands, gesturing that he was done. He stepped away, intercepted by Elena, who hugged his waist. "Huy, Bodhi. That temper of yours."

Agent Hughes approached and laid her hand on his shoulder. "I am truly sorry, Doctor. I thought you knew."

"I didn't … didn't know what happened to her after we jumped. What did you promise, Phillip?"

"Only that we would return him to an earlier time to rescue his wife if he fully cooperated with us."

Bodhi pointed at Hughes, darkness settling over his face. "Don't you allow that man to go anywhere near my mother. She's found peace, and you *will* respect that. Otherwise, you can count us out. If there's one thing I've learned about Phillip, he's responsible for her death."

"We had no intention of allowing that, I assure you. We were only using it to barter with him."

"And what are your intentions with us? Are you lying to Elena and me as well? … To barter?"

"No, Doctor. You and Elena are honorable people. As is Cassie. We need your help, and when we've accomplished our goal, you are free to return to your lives."

Elena butted in. "And what is your goal?"

"If you'll take a seat, I'll explain everything once Cassie arrives."

Cassie rushed to his side, snaking her arm around his. Elena gripped Bodhi's other arm, her palms moist against his skin. Clutching the arms of the two women he adores most in this world, he wondered how can he protect them? Maybe they can escape. The wheels in his mind spun like the fine-tuned gears of a Swiss watch.

Agent Hughes took the stage, standing in front of the pulsating triangle. She folded her hands and nodded.

"I don't want to waste any more time, so I'll get straight to the point of this first mission. One of many we hope." She stepped forward to the edge of the stage.

"Our first mission is to test the power of the Trinity to change the past … permanently. A subtle change, mind you, but something we can measure and prove that the past can be manipulated."

Bodhi interrupted. "Our experience is that the past cannot be changed. Or it can change for a time, then eventually correct itself."

Hughes stepped backward and rested her hand atop the Tempus Glass. "It's true that changes made in the past will correct themselves when trekking through time with *one* relic. But we've learned from the tome that trekking time with the power of the three allows history and destiny to be permanently changed."

Bodhi glanced at Elena, then Cassie, and back toward Hughes. "What could possibly go wrong?" He rolled his eyes and crossed his arms.

Hughes raised a calming hand. "Hear me out. We wish to test this theory on a small scale."

Elena interrupted. "Even the tiniest changes to fate can have devastating consequences on the present and future. We are not meant to play God. What you're proposing is irresponsible and dangerous."

"I appreciate your concerns, Elena. We've taken a serious look at the risks using the skills and knowledge of top risk management experts. We feel the risks are worth taking to expand our knowledge and better our circumstances as a species."

Cassie scoffed. "Seriously? You can't possibly understand the risks of what you're proposing. There are so many variables and measurables you cannot account for. The risk is high. Critical. And the outcome far too unpredictable. You're like children wanting to throw rocks at a hornet's nest … just to see what happens."

Hughes nodded and smiled. "One reason we feel your participation on the team is beneficial, Cassie. Your expertise in chemistry and the scientific method will be an invaluable asset to our study."

"I'm flattered, but it does nothing to calm my fears or answer my concerns. I want to read your risk management assessments and review your methods. What's your hypothesis? How are you collecting and crunching data?"

"That's not possible at this time, I'm afraid, Cassie. One parameter for this experiment is for the three of you to have limited knowledge to prevent that knowledge from influencing the outcome."

Bodhi interjected. "Sam, where are we going, and what is the goal here? In simple terms…"

Hughes' eyes widened over a beaming grin. "Thanks for asking, Doctor. The mission is simple. You must all concentrate on the morning of August seven, nineteen-forty-two, San Francisco, the Glen Five and Ten on the corner of Chenery and Diamond Streets."

Cassie asked, "Why? What's there?"

"To maintain the integrity of the experiment, that is all I can share with you at this time."

Cassie glanced at Bodhi and whispered, "I don't like this, dude. I don't trust them."

Bodhi chuckled. "Did you just call me, *dude*? I don't trust them either, Blondie. Let's bide our time until we figure out what they're up to."

"I agree with your papa, Mija. Let's see how everything plays out."

"If there are no further questions, please take your positions."

Cassie stood next to the Mariner's Compass while Bodhi and Elena stood next to the timepiece and Tempus Glass. They concentrated and chanted. Agent Hughes retreated from the stage and planted herself into a seat in row five.

Moments later, a dazzling vortex burst into the center of the stage within the triangle. The trio gripped the relics, held hands, and jumped.

TWELVE

They stepped onto the sidewalk on Diamond Street beneath a sapphire sky and a soft, salty breeze. Elena shivered, tucking herself inside the warmth of Bodhi's arms.

"Ay, I should have brought a warm coat. Tengo frío!"

Cassie pointed toward the Five and Ten. "Guys, I'm sorry, but I'm starving. Maybe they have some hot coffee or warm cocoa and one of those Honey Buns."

Elena shoved Bodhi aside and locked arms with Cassie. "I'm with you, Mija. Let's go."

"Wait, girls … we're on a mission here…"

"The mission can wait five minutes, Dad."

"Fine. Get me a bagel or something with cream cheese."

He leaned against a light pole and marveled at the newness of the 'old' buildings lining the streets. A soft mew caught his ear and piqued his curiosity. *What the heck?*

Cassie bumped him from behind and handed him a croissant with cream cheese and a steaming cup of coffee. "Here ya go, Pops. It's all they had."

He sipped the coffee and gnawed at the chewy crust—a burst of warm cream cheese filling his mouth. "The coffee is killer. Great idea, Blondie."

The mews grew louder and desperate.

He paused. "You girls hear that?"

Elena frowned, focusing on the sound. Her eyes widened with excitement. "Aw. It sounds like a gatita … a kitten."

Cassie peered down the mouth of a storm drain. "Oh, my God. It's just a baby. She's so adorable."

"How do you know it's a *she*, Blondie?"

"I … I just know."

"Alright, team. Let's roll. Not sure where we're going but…"

"Seriously, Dad? You're going to just leave her in there?"

"Cass. We're not here to save stray kittens—"

"Then what are we here for?"

"Well, I don't exactly know."

"Then how do you know it's not to save the kitty?"

"Come on, Blondie. You're joking, right?"

Elena punched his arm. "Bodhi. You can't leave that poor, helpless gatita stuck in there like that. Let's get her out first, then go."

He shrugged and shook his head. "Okay, I can see I'm outnumbered here." He leaned over and lifted the iron grid from the storm drain.

"Grab her," he grunted.

Cassie scooped the drenched, shivering kitten into her arms—her fur stained with mud. She returned to the store and reemerged with a fluffy cotton towel, the kitten's sparkling golden eyes wide and blinking.

"She's a white calico. I'm naming her Nixie … Aw, I can't stand it, you guys. She's so cute."

"It's nineteen forty-two, Cass. She already died."

"Dad! Seriously?"

Elena slapped his shoulder. "Bodhi."

"Or … maybe not. But we can't keep her, Blondie. Now, let's go."

An eight-year-old boy riding a bright red bicycle nearly crashed into them. Bodhi caught the bike by the handlebars, preventing a disaster.

"Ya might wanna slow down there, buddy."

The boy gazed up at Cassie. "Is that a kitty?"

Cassie leaned over. "It is. You want to pet her?"

The boy stroked Nixie's ears with a gentle touch, prompting soft mews.

"What's her name?"

"Nixie. What's yours?"

"Joey."

"Well, Joey, we have to go. Be more careful riding your bike, okay?"

"Okay." Joey rode away, glancing back at Cassie and grinning.

Cassie tapped Bodhi's shoulder with her fist and flashed a crooked smile. "Where to, Dad?"

He shrugged and pointed towards little Joey zipping away on his bike.

As they began their stroll along Diamond Street, tires screeched, twisted metal groaned, and the shrill of a woman's voice shrieked. The gnarled frame of little Joey's bicycle launched into the air without him.

Cassie shouted, "Oh my God! Dad!"

Winds swirled, tossing Elena's hair and blowing the hood off Cassie's head. A powerful vortex opened, blocking their path and sucking them into its gaping jaws.

Bodhi hollered, "Leave the kitten, Cass."

"No way!" Cassie bundled Nixie into a ball inside the blanket and drew her knees into her chest as they were swept away into silent darkness.

$$\approx$$

Agent Hughes and Agent Abara rose from their seats and greeted the trio as they stepped from the vortex onto the stage.

"Well done," Abara said.

Bodhi grimaced and cast a glance at Cassie and Elena. "What exactly did we do? That boy ... who was he? We need to go back."

Cassie stroked Nixie's head, stepping off the stage. "How do you mean? What happened to little Joey? What did you do?"

Hughes crinkled her brow and stretched her lips. "We're not sure yet." Hughes leaned into the kitten and stroked her whiskers. "Aw."

Bodhi and Elena stepped off the stage and joined Cassie. Bodhi gripped his right knee, nearly stumbling. "Ah. Damn it, man. My knee just locked up like a rusted crescent wrench. I've never had knee problems. What the hell?"

He glared at Hughes, then at Abara. "So, that's it? We're done for the day? No explanations, no reasons why? Do you even care that a little boy was killed or seriously injured?"

"The boy is irrelevant. A necessary casualty," Abara replied.

Hughes shot a scowl towards Abara and said, "You've permanently changed the present by interacting with the past." Hughes' hands quivered, and she fidgeted, pacing the floor.

Abara nodded and clamped his hands in front of a smug grin, as if praying. "Sam will escort you to your quarters until further notice."

Cassie stepped towards Abara. "Is that where my husband and son are waiting?"

Abara and Hughes gazed at one another, their stoic expressions raising concerns from the group. Hughes rested her hand on Cassie's shoulder. "I'm sorry ... you don't have a husband. Or a son, Cassie."

Cassie collapsed onto the edge of the stage. "W-what are you talking about? Of course I do. My husband, William ... and my son, Little William.

You've met them. What have you done … what have you done with them?"

Abara kneeled in front of Cassie, pressing the tips of his steepled fingers to his lips. He paused, inhaled, then tilted his head. "Cassie, we did nothing with them. The truth is, they do not exist. Let's move on."

Cassie screamed, her face reddening and her eyes darkening. "Take me to them! Now! Is this some kind of sick joke? Because it isn't funny." She lowered her head, pressing the tips of her fingers to her temples as she trembled from the shock of her alternate reality.

Bodhi grabbed Abara by the elbow and yanked him to his feet. "What the hell did you people do?"

Abara jerked his arm away and jammed a stern finger into Bodhi's sternum. "Do not put your hands on me, Mr. Johnson."

"Mr. Johnson? What the fu—"

Abara snapped his fingers and nodded toward the group. "Take them to the debriefing room."

Bodhi raised his palms. "Wait. Why? What the hell's going on?"

Agents swarmed the trio and dragged them into the hallway, forcing them into a twenty-by-twenty-foot room with sterile white walls and a single heavy wooden door. They sat in three metal chairs at a solitary stainless-steel table, waiting for answers.

Agent Hughes entered and tossed two manila folders on the table. She opened the first one.

"Mr. James Bodhi Johnson. Former All-American quarterback at UCLA and second-round draft pick of the San Francisco Forty-Niners … Spent seven years in the league. A three-time all-pro. Retired because of an ACL injury to his right knee. Turned to broadcasting for the NFL, making good use of his bachelor's degree in sports broadcasting and master's in communications. Currently, an English teacher and football coach at John Burroughs High School in Burbank, California. Divorced from Savanna Johnson. One daughter, Cassie Johnson."

His heart pounded into his throat. "What the hell? I guess that explains my knee."

Cassie shivered, hugged Nixie, and sobbed. "Daddy, what's happening to us?"

Hughes opened a second folder.

"Miss Cassie Johnson. Divorced from her high school sweetheart, Jacob Wallace. Graduated from USC with a bachelor's degree in chemistry and didn't complete her master's degree. Works as a chemical engineer at Rayon Semiconductor in Modesto, California.

Cassie whispered, "Oh, my God. I have memories of all of that. But none of it happened. Or did it?"

Hughes glanced at Elena and rested her palm on the table. "Nothing in your file has changed."

Bodhi pounded the table. "How did this happen? Somebody better start talking!"

"Calm down, Bodhi. Please—"

"I'm not going to calm down until you tell us what the hell is going on here. What created this ... nightmare? I knew we shouldn't have trusted you people. We need to go back to save that little boy. He's the key to all of this."

"What's done is done, Bodhi. I'm so sorry. You can't go back."

"Who was the boy? Sam ... who was the boy?"

She blinked rapidly and peered at the door. "I-I can't tell you. It would compromise the—"

"Damn it, Sam. Who was he? Please. A little boy was killed. Now, members of my family are missing."

Bodhi locked eyes with her. "I see the conflict in your eyes, Sam. You're troubled … You didn't expect this outcome either. Help us go back and fix this."

Agent Hughes nibbled her lower lip and broke his stare. Hesitating. Contemplating. "I can't," she whispered.

She stood, tucked the folders under her arm, and marched out of the room.

THIRTEEN

Bodhi, Elena, and Cassie entered a mid-sized, sparsely furnished apartment featuring two bedrooms and a bathroom. The click of the bolt left them alone and imprisoned. Bodhi plopped onto an easy chair while Elena stretched her legs across a leather sofa and sighed. Cassie slipped behind the kitchen island and leaned across the counter, popping the seal of a Vernor's ginger ale she found in the fridge.

"She's going to help us … I can feel it," Bodhi insisted.

"She won't help us. Guau, Bodhi, you're too trusting. You need to ignore your heart and listen to your brain."

Cassie gripped the soda can and pointed at Elena with her index finger. "No, maybe Dad's right. She seemed conflicted when we returned … almost shaken. As if she was trying to keep her crap together in front of Abara. It's obvious she's afraid of him."

"I hope you both are right. We need to save that poor niño. Our presence caused that accident. Had we not delayed him, he'd have lived out his life as he should. The question is … why did his death change the path of your lives?"

Cassie slurped her soda and tapped the can on the counter. "Exactly. I don't understand how little Joey is connected to us or how his death changed everything." Tears welled and gushed. "Daddy? I can't live without my baby ... or my William. This is so surreal ... I feel like I'm living in a horrible nightmare I can't wake up from."

She crumbled. Sliding down the wall into a fetal position. Bodhi leaped from his seat and crawled next to her, cradling her and guiding her head against his chest.

"It'll be alright, sweetheart. I'll fix this. Somehow, I'll fix it."

Cassie bear hugged him and wailed, her body trembling with sobs. Bodhi's heart broke from the depth of her anguish, helpless to mend what was broken inside his little girl. Anger rose in his throat. How dare they hurt her!

Elena squatted next to Cassie and kissed her hand. "Your papa is right, Mija. We'll find a way. No one can break us. Look what we've been through together. William and our precious niño are out there waiting in another timeline. We'll find them, I promise."

"Why are they doing this to us? Why can't they just let us go home?" Cassie wiped her cheeks with her palms. "I'm sorry, guys. I just needed a moment..."

A soft tap, followed by the clanks of bolts, drew their attention to the entrance. Samantha Hughes slipped inside, locking the door behind her. Her eyes widened, her face milky white, clutching a black leather briefcase in her right hand as if it were a time bomb handcuffed to her wrist.

Bodhi moved from one knee to standing upright, grunting and gripping his right knee. Elena guided Cassie to the sofa, sitting so close they seemed attached at the hip.

Bodhi gestured for Agent Hughes to join them. "I hope you're here to help us, and your motives are sincere, Sam."

"I could lose my badge for this," she muttered as she planted herself at the kitchen table. "Or worse."

"Who was the boy, Sam?" Bodhi asked.

Hughes opened the briefcase and slid on her glasses. "The boy was Joseph McMullin. The man your grandmother married, the man who gave you your name, and the man who helped raise you. Without his influence, you chose a different path in life. The ripples altered Cassie's life as well. She never went back in time. Never met William Cooper."

Cassie sniffled. "Oh, God. This is so frick'n unbelievable."

Bodhi leaned forward and folded his hands. "Sam, we have to go back and fix this. Will you help us? Please."

She nodded. "I came here to help correct this terrible mistake. But you can't return to the same moment of that timeline. You must enter through the moments before you arrived. That's very important."

"When can we leave?"

"It's not that easy. I have to smuggle you into the amphitheater on the next shift change. We'll have less than two minutes to act. Once inside, the cameras will spot you. I can't be seen with you."

Bodhi nodded and narrowed his eyes. "Understood. Sam, what's really going on here? What's Abara's end game?"

Hughes exhaled a ragged breath as she removed two data slides marked "Top Secret" from the briefcase.

"I shouldn't be telling you this. It could literally cost me my life. Sending you back to nineteen forty-two, San Francisco was never part of the plan. It caused the death of your step-grandfather and the rippling effects that followed. It's inexcusable."

Elena leaned forward and asked, "Why not report it to—"

"You don't understand the power and influence he carries. He has powerful politicians in his pocket. No one dares to challenge him."

"Then why risk helping us?" Cassie asked.

"Because it isn't right. I can't sit back and do nothing anymore. I want to help you fix this. Agent Abara is my boss and expects unquestioned loyalty. But I've found some of his actions unauthorized. Last week he had an agent, a good friend of mine, thrown into the brig for the crime of questioning one of his decisions. He never used to be like that."

"How do you mean?" Bodhi asked.

"He used to be kind, professional. Following the rules to the letter. Now he seems secretive. Elusive. And lately, very cruel."

Hughes removed a laptop from the briefcase and initiated a three-dimensional computer screen in front of the group.

"Have you heard of CERN and the Large Hadron Collider of the 2020s and the even larger hadron collider completed five and a half months ago?"

Bodhi stood, squinting at the collection of files, illustrations, and schematics floating in front of him.

"I've heard of the LHC of the 2020s, but I thought the bigger collider wasn't scheduled for release until the mid-2040s."

"They released it early and in secret."

Cassie asked, "How is this all related to Abara?"

Sam scooched her chair from the table, stood, and paced. "Back in the early 2000s, a lot was made of the Mayan calendar prophecy. The Mayan calendar ended on December 21, 2012. Many interpreted this to mean the end of the world—the apocalypse. Of course, it didn't happen. At least not in the way many expected."

Bodhi crinkled his brow. "How do you mean?"

"Do you recall the date the LHC confirmed the existence of the Higgs Boson particle? The *God Particle*, as they coined it."

Bodhi, Elena, and Cassie all glanced at one another. Bodhi shrugged. "I can't say that I do."

"It was July 4, 2012," Sam replied.

"So, what does that even mean?" Cassie snapped.

"Black holes. Unstable, microscopic black holes."

Sam swiped a virtual folder and isolated a government document in the center of the display.

"This black hole opened after the discovery of the God Particle and didn't close. Although microscopic, it was stable, held open by *exotic matter*. After a few days, it grew—extremely minimal growth, but detectable. Five months later, it grew exponentially and collapsed."

"And what's the significance of that? I'm not following." Bodhi said.

"Look at the date, Bodhi."

December 21, 2012.

"Alright. I see the connection to the Mayan prediction, but why is it important?"

"After the event of December 21, 2012, something strange happened. Remote viewers working for the government could no longer function. All timelines led to the same future—a point where they all converged. After that, the future couldn't be read anymore, so it became useless, and they shut their remote viewing projects down."

Bodhi shook his head in disgust. "Because they could no longer manipulate world events, so they had no use for the system anymore."

"Precisely."

Cassie wandered to the fridge and popped the top of another ginger ale. She sipped, squelched a belch, then asked, "So, why do you think they couldn't see the future anymore?"

"We believe our universe as we know it was destroyed by the black hole on December 21, 2012, fulfilling the Mayan prophecy, and it sent us into an alternate timeline in another universe. But no one noticed. The Mayans somehow understood."

"That's insane," Cassie replied. She scooped Nixie into her arms and plopped onto the sofa.

Hughes grimaced. "Maybe. Maybe not."

Bodhi guffawed. "I think you're reaching, Sam. That's silly."

Cassie interrupted, "It might explain the Mandela Effect so many people experience."

"Come on, Blondie. More nonsense."

Elena chimed in. "What is this *Mandela Effect*, Cassie?"

Cassie scooted next to Elena. "Nelson Mandela was some guy most people thought died in prison in the 1980s, but he actually died in 2013. Lots of people remember product names, logos, movie lines, and historical events wrong. A children's book titled 'The Berenstain Bears' was remembered by most as 'The *Berenstein* Bears.' I had that book growing up, and I swear it was *Berenstein*."

Bodhi clapped a hand to his forehead and grunted. "Come on, man. This is stupid. Enough with the Mandela Effect. People's memories of the Monopoly guy or underwear logos only demonstrate how bad our memories are."

Hughes closed her laptop and slid it into the briefcase. "We're in a time loop, Bodhi. Caused by the 2012 event. What's worse is that the newest Hadron Collider has created an intentional black hole. This one large enough to be observed by the human eye. It's terrifying."

"Seriously? For what purpose?" Cassie asked.

"Time travel … Time travel and a more sinister purpose—the use of dark matter to create a weapon so destructive and evil every government in the world could be wiped out in less than a second."

Bodhi's jaw slackened. "What the hell?"

"Thus, the reason our government wanted the relics. The end goal is to go back in time and change history, so CERN and the Hadron Collider never create a black hole and we were never sent to an alternate universe."

Bodhi heaved a breath. "So, why murder my grandfather in the process?"

"No reason at all. Abara wanted to test the theory that using all three relics in unison could change the past permanently and wipe out events.

Once that theory is proven, phase II of preventing the 2012 event and its effects can begin."

Hughes apologetically tilted her head and widened her misty eyes. "What Abara did was cruel and unnecessary. I had no idea what he was up to. I'm so sorry, Bodhi. He's taken charge of this entire project, and none of us knows the full details. Only Agent Abara has all the information."

"Apology accepted. We appreciate your help, Sam."

She checked her watch. "I have to go. I'll be back in two hours and twenty-three minutes. Be ready … all three of you."

The door swung open two feet, and an arm reached inside and waved, gesturing them to follow.

The three scurried into the hallway and shadowed Agent Hughes along the dim corridors to the amphitheater door. She heaved a breath, turned, and faced them. "Are you ready? Be quick," she whispered.

Hughes unlocked the door and disappeared into the darkness of an adjacent hallway. Bodhi, Elena, and Cassie rushed inside and stepped onto the stage.

Elena whispered, "Concentrate."

Within seconds, the door swung open and slammed against the wall.

"Freeze! Do not move a muscle. Step off the stage. Now!"

Four agents armed with stun weapons converged on them. Bodhi raised his arms and nodded at Elena and Cassie. "Do as they say. Stay completely still."

Agent Abara entered, forcing Samantha Hughes through the doorway, her hands cuffed behind her back.

"I'm very disappointed. Do you think I am unaware of everything that transpires inside this facility? You think me an imbecile?"

"Nobody thinks you're an imbecile, Abara. An asshole, yes, but not an imbecile. Let them go. This was all my idea," Bodhi insisted.

"A chivalrous gesture, Mr. Johnson … or do you wish to be addressed as Doctor McMullin? Technically, you're not a physician anymore."

"We need to go back, Abara. Where's your decency? Your humanity? You have your data; let us change things back."

"You can't go back, Bodhi. Not possible. I will not risk losing my *proof of concept* that the past can be permanently changed."

"We need to try. A boy's life is at stake, not to mention the repercussions of his death that you've inflicted on my family."

"You will do as I say, Bodhi, and since we're gathered here in this quiet hour, why not proceed with phase two of our mission?"

"Let my family go. I'm asking man-to-man … father to father."

"As you wish. Phase two will test your ability to control all three relics, sir. Are you up for the challenge?"

Abara twisted his body towards Agent Hughes and waved his fingers, dismissing her. "Take Ms. Hughes to isolation and confine her until I wish to deal with her. Go."

He pointed at Elena and Cassie. "Have a seat, ladies. Please."

Elena huffed. "Let us go with him. Why are you doing this?"

Abara chuckled. "Because. One set of footprints is far less invasive than three. Besides, your husband will surely complete the mission because he won't risk your safety while he's gone."

"Get on with it, Abara. Where am I going? What's the mission?" Bodhi grumbled.

"I'm delighted you asked. You are to travel to London on September 2nd, 1928. Saint Mary's Hospital, to be exact. The day before Sir Alexander Fleming discovered—"

Cassie interrupted. "Discovered penicillium mold in a Petri dish by accident. What are you people after?"

"If you will allow me to finish after so rudely interrupting me, I'll tell you."

Abara stepped toward Cassie. "What if the world never discovered penicillin? How would history have played out? What would happen to the world population?"

Cassie rose, cuddling Nixie and stroking her fur. "I'm going to stop you right there, Mr. Abara, or whatever your name is. The effects would be catastrophic. Are you proposing that my father go back in time and prevent the greatest discovery in medical science history? Are you out of your freaking mind?"

Bodhi shouted, "I won't be responsible for that!"

"I'm afraid you have little choice in the matter, *Mr. Johnson*. I have custody of your wife and daughter, and unless you do exactly as I say, there's no telling what might happen to them."

"You're threatening my family now? What's to say if I do this, *your* existence will be erased? You're willing to risk that?"

"Let's just say I know my family history. I am confident that it simply won't be the case. I have researched your family history and have calculated a 79.8 percent chance of your survival and an 81.3 percent chance for Cassie. Elena, fortunately, has a 100 percent chance. Those are manageable risks I'm willing to gamble on."

Bodhi seethed—his eyes narrowed. "You're *willing* to gamble on? That's the most ludicrous statement you've made all night. The only way I'd even consider it is if you allow me to go back to San Francisco, 1942, and restore my family history."

"You're not understanding me, Bodhi. There is no negotiation. Either you do what I ask, or you will never see your family again … or what's left of it. Am I clear?"

He heaved a breath and nodded. "Crystal."

"Good. Then, let us proceed. Concentrate on the mission. We will anxiously await your return."

Bodhi stood in the center of the Triad and sang, stimulating the emerald band of light connecting the relics. A powerful vortex engulfed him like a whirlpool of colorful clouds and dazzling lights, swallowing him before vanishing. Moments later, Bodhi returned and collapsed onto the stage. Cassie and Elena rushed onto the platform, helping him to his feet and guiding him to a seat.

Abara initiated a large three-dimensional computer screen and sorted through data like a necromancer sorting through a spell book.

"This is fascinating. The world population was reduced from 8.7 billion to 6.3 billion—a reduction of roughly 2.4 billion souls. Penicillin wasn't discovered for another twenty-seven years. A group of German scientists made the find. There is no mention of Alexander Fleming anywhere in the history books."

A soldier guarding the exit answered a knock at the door. A young woman whispered something in his ear, then disappeared, closing the door behind her.

"Agent Abara, sir, Samantha Hughes has escaped her cell."

Abara tapped a search on his keyboard, rubbing the stubble on his chin, and chuckled. "Agent Hughes didn't escape ... That'll be all, private."

Bodhi whispered, "We need to jump. We have to fix this."

Elena clasped her hand over his. "Bodhi, distract him."

"Why? What are you going to do?"

"Just distract him."

Bodhi approached Abara. "I just have one question ..."

"Fire away, sir."

"Do I have your word not to hurt my family if I do what you ask?"

"Most certainly."

Bodhi extended his hand. "Then we have a deal."

The second Abara gripped his hand, Bodhi yanked him forward and head-butted him, tackling him to the floor. Elena raced toward the stage.

A searing jolt of electricity shot up Bodhi's spine like the kick of a mule. He rolled into a fetal position and groaned. Cassie dropped Nixie and leaped onto the soldier's back, clawing at his eyes and screeching like a wild banshee.

Elena grasped the Tempus Glass and chanted. An emerald mist filled the room, freezing Abara and the soldier. Bodhi rolled away from the stun beam, gasping and grunting. Cassie slid off the soldier and glanced toward Elena, stunned. "What did you do?"

Elena smiled. "A little trick I learned."

Bodhi pushed himself off the ground and stumbled toward the stage. Elena gripped the Tempus Glass, Bodhi held the timepiece, and Cassie snatched the Mariner's Compass.

"Where are we going first?" Cassie asked.

Bodhi winked. "San Francisco, 1942. We have a young boy to rescue and a family name to restore."

"Wait a second." Cassie tucked Nixie into the kangaroo pocket of her UCLA hoodie and leaped onto the stage. "I'm ready, guys."

FOURTEEN

Bodhi, Elena, and Cassie stepped onto the sidewalk on Diamond Street in 1942, San Francisco. Cassie reached inside the kangaroo pocket of her hoodie and panicked. "Where is she? Where's Nixie? I had her a second ago."

Bodhi pointed at the storm drain with his eyes and sighed. He lifted the iron grid while Cassie rescued Nixie a second time.

"Wait here, guys." Cassie returned three minutes later with Nixie swathed inside a cotton towel, wet behind the ears, and blinking at the world like a newborn.

Elena shivered. "Warm me up, Corazón. Or steal me a coat."

They huddled against the side of the Five and Dime, guarded from the bite of the wind. Cassie planted herself on the curb, glancing down the sidewalk every few minutes for a little boy on a red bike.

Half an hour later, Joey McMullin pedaled furiously, head down, huffing and puffing like a boy on a mission. Bodhi stepped out of the shadows and grabbed Joey's handlebars, forcing an abrupt stop.

"Whoa, whoa, slow down, buddy."

"Hey, mister. I'm not supposed to talk to strangers. And I'm in a hurry…"

"Where's the fire, son?"

114

"I'm headed to my pal, Jackie's house … to show him my new bike. Can I go, sir? Please?" His eyes widened and blinked, gazing up at Bodhi.

Cassie kneeled next to Joey and unraveled the towel. Joey's eyes popped, and his jaw hung. "Gosh. Is that a kitty?"

"It sure is."

"What's her name?"

"Nixie. You want to pet her?"

"Can I? That's mighty swell of ya."

"She needs a new home, Joey. You want to—"

"Saaay … how'd you know my name?"

"Lucky guess. Or maybe because someone wrote your name on this piece of tape stuck to your bike … duh." Cassie playfully lifted Joey's ball cap and mussed his hair. "So, what do you say, Joey? Do you want to take care of Nixie for me? Take her home and give her lots of love…"

"Gee, I don't know. My mom ain't gonna like it."

"Come on … take her home, buddy. Your friend can wait, and your mom is going to love Nixie. You'll see."

"Ha … you don't know my mom."

Cassie unfolded a five-dollar bill and stretched it, grinning ear to ear. "I'll give ya five bucks."

Joey's eyes lit up, gazing at the bill. "Okay, swell. I'll take her home.

"Great. We'll follow you, and I'll carry Nixie until we get there."

They followed Joey for a block and a half down Chenery Street to a tiny two-story home with blue shingles, white trim, and a miniature porch.

Bodhi whispered, "I remember seeing pictures of this house in my grandpa's photo albums. Man…"

Bodhi kneeled next to Joey and shook his hand. "You take care, little buddy. Remember to feed that cat."

A random thought popped into Bodhi's mind. *What if taking care of Nixie was a factor in why Joey grew up to be such a loving dad and grandpa? Maybe Joey was supposed to find Nixie all along, helping him avoid the accident.*

Cassie giggled. "I can't believe that's Grandpa Joe." She wrapped her arms around Bodhi's waist and rested her head on his heart. "What now, Dad?"

"Well, before the Five and Dime realizes you paid them with money not printed yet, we should head back to Saint Mary's Hospital in London—the day before, Fleming returns from vacation."

"Just curious, Pops ... What'd you do with the Petri dish?"

"I hid it on top of a cabinet."

"What? You put it on top of a cabinet?" Cassie rolled her eyes and shook her head.

"Well, it worked, didn't it?" Bodhi grumbled.

"Apparently so, Doctor. Brilliant move." She snickered.

"Where would you have hidden it, Blondie? In the ladies' room?"

"Somewhere other than the top of a cabinet. It doesn't matter. We need to hurry and get the heck out of here."

Elena chuckled. "There's no hurry, Mija. They can't follow us anymore. We're free, and after we've returned history to its proper place, we'll return these relics to their proper owner."

Cassie's face drained of color. She gasped. "Dad? Elena? I just realized something. Saving Grandpa Joe means we saved my family. Oh, God ... William and the baby are back in the room ... in the government facility. What do we do?"

"Calm down, Blondie. We can time travel, remember? We'll go back and get them."

Cassie's voice quivered. "You really think they're there? What if Abara and his thugs are waiting for us? What if they use William and the baby as collateral?"

Elena gripped Cassie's hand. "They can't handle all three of us, Mija. The powers we wield are like nothing in this universe. You worry too much." She patted her hand.

Cassie inhaled sharply. "Okay … You're right. We've got this. Let's hold hands and chant."

They traveled through the vortex and entered a dimmed lab at Saint Mary's Hospital. Cassie's expression was akin to a kid discovering Santa's workshop. She moved about the lab, lips parted, stretching her fingertips within inches of antique beakers, test tubes, surgery tools, chemical compounds, and preserved specimens floating in jars like a sideshow at a carnival. The place was a living museum.

"Oh, my God. This is where it happened, guys. Where penicillin was discovered. I always pictured it wrong in my head. My kitchen is bigger than this."

Bodhi brushed his hand over the top of one cabinet, stirring up a cloud of dust. He slapped his palm across the cabinet like a man looking for his keys. "Aw, shit. Where is it? I'm sure I put it right here."

"Maybe it was this one over here, Bodhi."

"No, I'm positive it's this one."

"Then it should be there. Look again."

Bodhi reached further back, the tips of his fingers brushing across an object. He grunted. "Maybe this is it." The object slid forward from the prodding of his wriggling fingers and crashed to the tile floor, shattering into hundreds of shards.

He glanced toward Elena and Cassie with widened eyes, his mouth agape, and his hand still raised over the cabinet. Cassie covered her mouth and whispered, "Oops."

"¡Venga! Bodhi. You're like a horse in the kitchen."

"Damn it, what do we do?"

Cassie brushed away the broken glass and scooped several samples of the blue-green mold. "Quick, get me another Petri dish. Dad! Move it."

Bodhi scrambled, bumping into tables and knocking over equipment. Elena slapped his arm. "¡Por Dios! Bodhi. Get out of the way." Elena snatched a Petri dish filled with agar. "Here, Mija."

Cassie took the dish and smeared the penicillium mold over the fresh agar, then spread the bacterial culture next to it. "That should do it. It just needs some time to grow."

"We need to get the hell out of here, girls."

Bodhi ripped a blank piece of paper from a notebook and snatched a pencil from a mason jar. He scribbled a note and slapped it on the tabletop next to the Petri dish.

"Dad. Seriously? You're leaving him a note?"

Cassie snatched the note and glanced at it. "*Check that one?* And you took the time to draw an arrow? Oh my God, Dad." Cassie rolled her eyes and crumpled the note, tossing it at him.

He caught the crumpled note, flipped it into a garbage pail, and shrugged. "Too obvious, huh?"

"Waaay too obvious. I promise he'll discover it without your fancy little arrow. Can we please rescue my family now? My neck is tingling."

They stepped through the portal into the apartment's main room inside the government facility. Cassie darted from room to room, her heart racing and her throat constricting.

"William? William, where are you?"

Elena grabbed Cassie's elbow. "Quiet, Mija. I don't think they're here."

"No. No, no, no. How are we going to find them? I knew it … I fricking knew this was going to happen. We're too late." She covered her heart with a quivering hand.

"We're not too late, Cass. We just need to figure out where they are."

"How, Dad? How do we do that? Where do we even begin?"

Elena snapped her fingers, grasped Cassie's hands, and guided her to the couch. "Cassie? When you returned to Gram's beach house with your little niño, you told us the baby opened the vortex, not you."

Cassie gasped; her eyes grew wide. She cupped her hand over her mouth and heaved an excited breath. "That's right. I didn't open it. I'm positive the baby did."

Bodhi shook his head, raked his fingers through his disheveled hair, and plopped on the couch beside them. "What's all that mean? I mean, what are you getting at, babe?"

Elena craned her neck toward Bodhi and beamed. "It means our little niño is connected to the timepiece like her madre and abuelo. We follow the echoes, Cariño."

Bodhi clapped and pointed. "Of course. Quantum entanglement."

Elena crinkled her brow. "Sí … that too."

They spent the next five minutes concentrating on quantum echoes radiating from the timepiece, pinging to a location hundreds of feet below them. When the time was right, the vortex opened and transported them into a vast, dim warehouse filled with crates, tools, storage shelves, forklifts, rolls of cable, and an 8 x 10 locked storage unit curiously sitting in the center of the concrete floor.

Cassie rushed to the storage unit and rapped on the door, wiggling the padlock. "William? Are you in there? William," she whispered.

A muffled voice responded, "Cass? Is that you?"

119

"Yes, Cappie, it's me. I'm here with Dad and Elena. We're going to get you out of there."

"They locked us in an hour ago. They're up to something. Be careful, Cass."

Bodhi nudged Cassie aside and clobbered the padlock with a ten-pound sledge, shattering it into pieces. He ripped the door open, slinging it against the wall. William stepped out, cradling the baby, whose wails echoed off the walls. Cassie kissed William on the lips and cuddled the baby, taking him from his father's arms. "It's okay, pumpkin, Mommy's here, now."

Bodhi rubbed his right knee and pursed his lips. "It's gone."

"What's gone, Dad?"

"My knee injury ... from football. Saving Grandpa Joe means I never injured my knee. Never played pro sports. And it's never felt better."

The back of Bodhi's neck tingled, and the hair on his forearms raised. Blue lightning crackled before he could even open his mouth, as a titanic shockwave thrashed them like a blast of dynamite. His world ... their world, went black.

FIFTEEN

Muffled voices and the drone of a vent fan roused him to consciousness. His temples throbbed, and his tongue stuck to the roof of his mouth. Every swallow scraped like gravel down his throat.

Bodhi peered at the ceiling, quickly squeezing his eyes shut from the piercing white light that stabbed the back of his skull like a hot iron. His spine ached from the middle of his shoulders down to the tip of his tailbone. He rolled on his side, planted his bare feet on a frigid floor, and buried his face in his palms.

"What the hell happened to us?" he mumbled.

Bodhi stood and stumbled forward, catching himself on the concrete wall. He squinted, using the walls to navigate his cell. The squeal of a speaker sent him backwards, plopping him on the cot. He clamped his hands over his ears and shouted, "Abara! You asshole! Where am I? Where's my family?"

The lights dimmed. "Good evening, Doctor McMullin. Your family is quite safe with me. They're fit and resting from their long journey. You, on the other hand, appear to be suffering a terrible hangover."

"That happens a lot when you're around. I want to see my family."

"In time, you can reunite with your family. For now, you'll do what I require of you."

"And what is that? Prevent the polio vaccine from being created? Help Hitler defeat the Allies?"

"Travel back to December 21, 2012, and prevent the black hole event that destroyed our universe and changed our timeline."

"I'm a medical doctor, not a scientist."

"You underestimate yourself, Bodhi. We've implanted an experimental chip developed by Neuralink inside your brain—"

"You did what?"

"Now, calm down. It's perfectly safe and you'll find the results fascinating, I'm sure."

"How about we plant one in your head and see how fascinating that is? Take it out. Now!"

"Well, that could be terribly risky, Bodhi, and in time, I'm confident you'll realize how necessary and beneficial it is."

Bodhi massaged his temples. "I need water … and food."

A slot in the wall opened, depositing a metal tray holding a bowl of steaming soup, a hard roll, and a water bottle. Bodhi guzzled the water and dipped the roll into the soup. "Thank you."

"You're quite welcome. Now, how about we test your knowledge of quantum physics?"

"What do you mean?"

"Exactly what I said. Concentrate on the laws of physics and quantum theory. Let us evaluate the level of knowledge you possess through your Neuralink implant. You might surprise yourself."

Complex scientific concepts flooded his mind like a major software download. Superposition, entanglement, wave-particle duality, every known concept of physics. Bodhi hit his knees, his ears ringing and his skull exploding with fire. He clamped his hands over his skull and groaned.

"Relax, Doctor. Breathe. Try not to think … calm your mind and concentrate."

"That's easy for you to say," he grunted as he rolled into a fetal position, wincing. "Take it out! I want it out of my head … something's not right."

"It's simply an unexpected side-effect, Bodhi. Disconnect your thoughts. Take your mind somewhere else."

"I can't."

"Try, Doctor. You must learn to control it, or—"

"Or what?"

"Or your brain function could shut down permanently."

Bodhi sipped short, quick breaths, rubbing his temples, and taking his mind to Stinson Beach, watching Cassie as a little girl playing with her puppy in the wet sand. The stabbing pain and waves of pulsating agony gradually faded. He sat upright and placed his head between his knees, waiting for his racing heart to slow.

"That's much better, Doctor. Control is key."

Bodhi raised a fist and extended his middle finger.

"I know this is difficult, but you'll need this knowledge to help understand how to close the black hole and restore our original universe."

The slot in the wall reopened, and the ancient Tome of Cassiel was put on the shelf next to his tray.

"You'll need to study the tome before you attempt such a feat. When you have fully prepared yourself, you will journey back to 2012 escorted by two of my agents and complete the mission."

"And if I refuse?"

"Then you and your wife will die, and your daughter will assume the mission."

"You're unbelievable, Abara. You'd murder innocent people to get what you want?"

"I'm afraid I have you by the balls, as you Americans say. Get busy, Doctor. That tome will not read itself. You have quite the demanding task ahead of you. If you want to see your family again, consider fully preparing yourself. Failure isn't an option, and may I remind you, Cassie is on deck."

Bodhi shuffled toward the tome, running his palm over the dusty cover, revealing the intricate artwork and engraved lettering. He lifted the ancient opus, squatted on the edge of the cot, and unlocked its pages. The secrets within the tome held the keys to the welfare of his family and their freedom. Extracting them wasn't optional.

"We'll work on your knowledge of physics tomorrow. For now, enjoy some fine reading. Your life and the lives of your family heavily depend on it. I'm sorry it has to be this way, but much is at stake. Good evening, sir."

Bodhi scoured the ancient writings throughout the night, sleeping for short periods. It kept his mind off the brain implant and focused his energy on studying the relics and how to rid the world of them. Time eluded him. His heart thumped with exhaustion.

Bodhi flinched from the crackle of static. "Good morning. How are your studies coming along, Doctor? I'm confident an entire world of understanding has revealed itself to you. Are you ready to save our universe?"

"Not hardly."

"Let's concentrate on the laws of physics again."

"Let me say this loud and clear. Hell no."

"We'll proceed slowly. Baby steps, as they say."

"Not doing it. I have no desire to experience the migraine from hell a second time."

"We've adjusted some things while you slept."

"Adjusted some things? You opened my skull again?"

"No, no. And we never opened your skull. Our adjustments were made remotely. We've lowered the I.Q. setting and implemented some safeguards in the data you can access. May we try again?"

"I don't trust you assholes."

"Please try again. Let's begin with the basic principles of entanglement and move on from there."

"How about no?"

"Doctor McMullin ... the world is counting on you. Your family is counting on you. The knowledge base contained within the Neurolink chip is vital to your success. It requires practice and discipline to master."

Bodhi heaved a breath and concentrated. He monologued a short dissertation on basic quantum entanglement. The principles were child's play in his thought process. The ringing in his ears returned, and his temples throbbed. Pinching the bridge of his nose held the migraine at bay for several seconds before the pain crashed into his skull like a freight train.

Bodhi cradled his head in his hands and bellowed. "My head is exploding. Get it out, please. I can't control it."

"Be calm, Bodhi. Take deep breaths and divert your thoughts."

Classic piano music resonated throughout his cell—the vibrations surprisingly easing the pressure inside his cranium.

"Excellent. Focus on the music. Let's try again."

"Try again? Are you crazy? I can't."

"You can and you will, Doctor. You must master this skill. Now, focus and tell me about superposition."

The moment his thoughts veered to superposition, the pounding resumed. His temples throbbed, and his eye sockets pulsed, blurring his vision. He collapsed onto the cot, pressing his fingers to his temples.

"Focus, Doctor. Our time is limited. We must move forward with the mission tomorrow. You must be ready."

Bodhi nodded and exhaled. "Tomorrow? Are you kidding?"

He exhaled and shook his head. "Okay, okay. I'll be ready. But before I do, I want to spend time with my family. You owe me that much."

"Fair enough. I'll arrange dinner with you and your family within the hour, and in the morning at precisely 6:00 a.m., you will begin your journey. Welcome aboard, Bodhi. I am pleased to have you on our team, finally.

A table for five was set with fine china, crystal goblets, and polished silverware, inside an intimate patio beneath a trillion stars and an amber harvest moon rising on the horizon. The night was balmy, the air filled with the sweet scent of orange blossoms. Bodhi sat alone. Waiting—drumming his fingers across the white linen of the tabletop.

A darkened glass door slid open. "Oh, Mi Corazón! Te amo mucho. Te he extrañado." Elena leaped into his arms, cradling his face and leaving bright red lip marks all over his cheeks.

"I love you, too, sweetheart. And I've missed you more." Bodhi's eyes misted. A lump the size of a melon lodged in his throat as his family filed onto the patio to greet him.

Elena has never looked more stunning. Her radiance in the soft moonlight and flickering candlelight mesmerized him. She gazed at him, her fiery emerald eyes filled with adoration. Her black evening gown clung to her full figure, highlighting her busty cleavage and driving his libido to the edge of insanity. He slid a chair out and seated her like a queen.

Cassie stood back with the baby on her hip and William's arm around her waist. Her brows raised to a peak, and her eyes glistened as she witnessed the depth of Bodhi and Elena's love for each other. "Aw, they're so cute together," she whispered to William.

Bodhi spread his arms and twirled Cassie and the baby in a half circle before setting them down.

"Ah, Blondie…" He choked up, unable to finish his sentence, then kissed her forehead and stole Little William from her arms.

"Man, you are as solid as a rock, little buddy. Papa has missed you so much."

Bodhi cradled the baby in his left arm and extended his right hand toward William. "Good to see you, Will. Thank you for taking care of my family all these weeks."

William nodded and gripped Bodhi's hand, pulling him in for a hug. "They're my family too, sir. It's my honor." William smacked Bodhi on the back and pointed towards the table. "I could eat a mule right now. Let's break bread and catch up on current events."

They dined on the most tender prime rib he'd ever tasted. Crisp, steamed asparagus, a loaded, fluffy baked potato, a rich avocado and tomato salad, and a thick slice of German chocolate cake, not to mention a thousand-dollar bottle of wine.

Bodhi pushed his plate to the side and scooped small slices of cake with his fork, savoring every bite. When he finished, he turned his fork over and folded his hands. His cup was full. But not with wine.

He broke the awkward silence around the table like a twig snapping beneath his feet in a silent forest. "I leave at six in the morning."

Elena grasped his hand and kissed his knuckles. "I believe in you, Mi Amore. I know you will return to us. You don't know how to fail."

"Daddy, please be careful. We'll be here—waiting for you—praying for your safety.

William laid his arm over Cassie's shoulders and squeezed her. "I've got things handled here, Bodhi. No worries, pal. Focus on the mission and come back safe. Then let's all get the heck out of here and take a swell vacation."

Bodhi pointed at William and winked. "Australia. Always wanted to go to Australia." He glanced at Cassie and grinned. "Blondie, you're in charge of planning it out. Two weeks in the outback."

Cassie dabbed her eyes with her napkin and sniffled. "I'm on it, buddy. It'll be the best vacation yet."

Two agents entered the patio at midnight and signaled Bodhi to follow them. He dabbed the corners of his mouth and swallowed.

"I guess this is it, fam." He rose and stepped towards the agents before Elena tugged on his wrist. She grasped his hand and placed a large emerald ring in his palm—Gram's ring.

"I want this back, Mi Amore. Promise?"

Bodhi nodded and stiffened his chin. He lifted Elena from her seat into his arms and planted a kiss on her lips, deep, wet, and intensely sexy. Cassie covered the baby's eyes and glanced at William. "O.M.G., guys … get a room."

Bodhi wrapped his long arms around Cassie, William, and the baby and squeezed. "I love you, Blondie. Take care of yourselves until I get back." As he walked through the exit, he glanced over his shoulder at the pained faces of his family, his heart pounding, and his insides churning.

SIXTEEN

Bodhi loomed on the stage inside the amphitheater, the three relics hovering above his outstretched palms, two armed agents next to him. His stomach fluttered like pre-game jitters. Abara rose from the shadows and stepped into the light.

"Destiny awaits, Doctor. You have your credentials. Doctor Andre Schwartz will await your arrival. We confirmed his journey back in time yesterday after his encrypted message from 2012 appeared on our server this morning. If all goes well, he'll get you in the room."

Bodhi pointed at the agents. "What about Hanz and Franz here? How do I explain them?"

"If you're referring to the agents accompanying you, their job is to escort you to the front door. They won't enter the CERN facility. Your job is to locate the black hole. And when you do … close it."

"What's to say, another black hole won't develop?"

"Hopefully, you did your homework. The welfare of your family depends on it."

The agents gripped their weapons, glaring nervously at one another as the vortex opened and swallowed them.

≈

Bodhi scaled the steps to CERN's entrance. He quickly glanced over his shoulder at the agents before slipping through the glass doors into the lobby unaccompanied.

A receptionist with round black-rimmed glasses and a tight brunette ponytail greeted him. "May I help you, sir?"

"Uh, yes. I'm a guest of Dr. Schwartz … um, here are my credentials. Can you let him know I'm here?"

"Of course, sir. Please have a seat."

Bodhi squatted onto an orange leather sofa and snatched the June 2012 edition of the CERN Courier magazine off the coffee table, flipping through the pages like an expectant father. An article about a black hole feasting on a stellar core caught his eye. Before he could skim through the highlights, a gentle voice with a slight German accent interrupted his thoughts.

"Doctor McMullin?" A short, thin man with gray, thinning hair and dark bushy brows, dressed in a casual black suit, extended a nervous hand toward him. Bodhi tossed the magazine on the table and rose to face him.

"I am Dr. Andre Schwartz. I vill escort you to za main auditorium to join za other scientists," he whispered in a thick German accent.

"Pleasure is mine, Andre. Call me Bodhi."

Andre led him down a long hallway, through several security checks, into the auditorium. They slid through the aisle of a lower balcony, finding two empty seats towards the end. A large white screen hung over the stage, awaiting the big announcement.

Andre leaned into Bodhi and muttered, "Our data shows za black hole opened seconds after za Higgs boson discovery vas announced. Act quickly ven zat happens. Godspeed, Doctor." Andre rose, placed his hand on Bodhi's shoulder, then shuffled through the aisle and exited the auditorium.

The announcement came. Applause erupted—not the kind born from performance, but the visceral reaction of minds witnessing the culmination of decades of theory, failure, and persistence.

Bodhi slipped the timepiece from his pocket, his chants muffled beneath the roars and commotion. As quickly as it erupted, silence blanketed the auditorium. Scientists were caught mid-sentence, others frozen in time. He removed the Tempus Glass and the Mariner's Compass and continued to chant, activating the bond of the three.

Bodhi knew what he had to do. He understood the risks. Before the 2012 black hole could consume his universe like a ravenous beast, Bodhi summoned the combined powers of the relics and focused his thoughts on his enhanced knowledge and the Trinity.

Complete understanding of quantum mechanics crashed into his mind like a raging river through a crumbling dam. His ears roared inside his head like a siren in a tornado, splitting his skull like a fireman's axe. He dropped to his knees, struggling to control the relics, shrieking from the intense shockwaves pulsating through his brain.

Holding on was impossible; blood gushed from his nostrils, and his heart raced out of his chest. He was dying. He knew it. Bodhi closed his eyes and gritted his teeth, awaiting his heart's final beat. A voice pierced the chaos. Gram's emerald ring glowed on his finger.

"James. Wake up. Use your voice, dear boy. The chords!"

Bodhi lifted his eyes. "Gram?"

"The chords, James. Use the power of your voice, grandson."

He sang as loudly and as poetically as he could muster. The relics reacted to his voice, returning vibrations and pitch to match his refrain. The vibrations transformed into the most beautiful music he'd ever experienced. It flowed through him like a heavenly choir, filling his soul with ecstasy and peace.

The heavens opened before him, revealing a tiny, growing black hole. Bodhi focused the power of the relics towards the celestial object. He was one with the relics—one with the universe. The pain was gone.

A single thought evaporated the black hole before it could burst into existence, nullifying the Mayan prediction—permanently changing destiny. The heavens closed like smoke sucked through a vent. He collapsed.

In an instant, the roars and applause resumed. The Higgs boson field was revealed and proven—a discovery that would redefine our understanding of creation, and a sign that it was time for him to leave.

Bodhi gathered the relics and crawled to his feet. He strolled through the lobby and dashed out the front door. An agent met him at the bottom of the steps, his glance focused over Bodhi's shoulder, towards the entrance, as if expecting a security team in pursuit.

Bodhi grabbed the agent's shoulder. "Where's Franz?"

"What?"

"Your partner … where's your partner?"

The agent scowled and shrugged. "It's just you and me, Doc. No partners."

"Damn it. Here we go again."

"Not sure what you mean, sir."

"Let me ask you a question. Bernstain, or Bernstein?"

"What? I, uh…"

"Bernstain Bears, or Bernstein Bears? It's a children's book."

"Oh, uh … *Bernstein.*"

"That's what I thought. Our work is done here."

≈

Bodhi and the agent stepped onto the stage, back inside the amphitheater. He set the relics on the pedestals and glared at Abara, shaking his head. "We're missing 'Franz'. Something changed."

"Have a seat, Doctor. Much has changed," Abara replied.

The grim look on Abara's face was unsettling. Bodhi slid into a nearby seat and ran his fingers through his hair. "What catastrophe did your meddling cause this time, Agent Abara?"

Abara appeared shaken. "History changed. Quite drastically, I'm afraid. I didn't anticipate this, I must admit."

"Well, this should be a fascinating debriefing. Before you begin, I want to know that my family is okay."

"They are well, Doctor. I assure you."

"All of them? Everyone accounted for?" Bodhi demanded.

"Your wife, daughter, her husband, and your grandson are all well and accounted for, *Doctor McMullin*."

Bodhi nodded and sighed. "Then let's continue. I'm afraid to ask, but … What's the weather like outside?

"December 21, 2012, marked the beginning of a limited nuclear war that broke out in the Middle East. Iran detonated a nuclear weapon on Israeli soil, and the response was devastating. A counterattack was launched, decimating most of Iran. Others joined the war against Israel. Syria, Iraq, North Korea, Turkey, Russia … the West came to the aid of Israel, and World War Three was underway."

Bodhi rubbed his temples and sighed. "The day the Mayan calendar ended. Tell me. When did the war end?"

"The war lasted nearly four years, Doctor. The world, as you remember, no longer exists."

Bodhi smacked his fist inside his other hand and rose. "What the hell did I tell you people? I warned you idiots what would happen if you messed with history."

"Indeed, you did. Which is why we must—"

Bodhi shoved a finger into Abara's face. "Must what? Go back? Something destroyed our old timeline, a divine power, or a big coincidence, I don't know which. But being sent to an alternate timeline by the 2012 event saved our world. You screwed up, Abara, and everything that's happened since is blood on your hands. This is the world your wife and your sons must now live in. A world, a tiny black hole in 2012, saved us from … until you changed it."

"It's unfortunate, Doctor. We had no means to predict the outcome or foresee the consequences," he sighed.

"Losing billions of lives and the radioactive contamination of cities, states, and even entire countries resulted in a new world order."

Bodhi plopped into an amphitheater seat and buried his face inside his hands. He raised his eyes and glared at Abara. "This is how you planned to protect our country? Our world? For the betterment of mankind? This was your goddam plan?"

Abara lowered his eyes. "No. This wasn't the plan. However, the future is promising, with the reduction in world population, the destruction of the world's nuclear arsenal, and the new world order. We all live under one governing body. No more governments. No more wars."

"What are you talking about? Have you lost your flipping mind?"

Abara shook his head and wagged a judgmental finger. "This was our destiny, Doctor. We corrected the universe's error created by the 2012 event and reset history back to its original timeline. We've succeeded, thanks to you. Now the remnants of humanity can rebuild society under the guidance of our leadership, and we can return to an age of innocence. A golden age where we are all equal and work together as one."

Bodhi rolled his eyes and threw up his hands. "You've lost your mind, buddy. This whole thing wasn't about securing the relics; it was always about power, control, and world domination. Setting yourself up as a world ruler … a king … or in your case, a god."

"Not hardly, Doctor. When Adam and Eve inhabited Eden, they were innocent. They existed in paradise. God allowed them complete freedom and gave them everything they needed as long as they never ate from the Tree of Knowledge. The Triad is that tree, Bodhi. We will guard its fruit from ever revealing its secrets."

Bodhi scoffed. "So, let me get this straight. You're God, and whoever is left outside living on a scorched planet are the new Adams and Eves? Well, I have news for you, bud. Your ambitions of a utopian society where people frolic naked in the sun all day while you play, God, ain't happening on my watch."

"It's a metaphor, Bodhi. Humanity that survives this war will work together as equals. Share in the toils and the riches to build a new and better world, free of war, disease, crime—"

"Communism. You want to install communism and become Stalin."

"You are shortsighted, Doctor. The world is on a collision course with extinction if we do not act. We have the power at our disposal to reverse those trends. People are starving, resources are dwindling, and nations in turmoil have joined as one entity. Technology has exploded over the past several decades, and it isn't being used in our best interest. We can make a difference, sir. Work *with* us instead of *against* us. Take your seat at the table, my friend."

"That's a brilliant speech, Abara. I'm not buying it. There's a whole lot of information missing here. The power you wish to wield is far more devastating and terrifying than any in the world today."

Abara exhaled a deep sigh and lowered his eyes. "Very well. Your mission is now complete, and your services are no longer needed. I will escort you to your family. You'll have the option to choose where to live out the rest of your lives in history."

"Booting us out of Eden, huh? The apples are rotten in your paradise, Agent. I'll take my family and go, but I'm taking the relics with me. You've taken your last bite of the apple."

Abara glanced at the guard and nodded. Electricity fired along Bodhi's spine like a hot wire, collapsing him to the floor. He groaned and crawled toward the stage, pulling himself upward. Air left his lungs as the agent's foot crashed into his ribs and cold steel cuffed his wrists.

Abara clicked his tongue and scoffed. "Why can't we do things the easy way, Doctor?" He glanced at the guard and snapped his fingers. "Get him out of here. Take him back to his family. Have Phillip meet me here in twenty minutes."

Bodhi heaved a breath and concentrated, straining a faint chant, stimulating the timepiece, now vibrating and singing back to him.

Abara shouted, "Grab the relics!"

Abara turned toward Bodhi and froze. The guard froze mid-step. Bodhi used the rail encircling the stage to pull himself to his feet and snag the key from the guard, unlocking his cuffs and allowing them to clamber against the floor. He snatched Abara's passkey and gathered the relics. Darting out the door, he sprinted through the hallway towards the apartment, where he prayed his family would await his return.

The door clicked as he slid the passkey over the sensor. Cassie stood in the kitchen with the baby on her hip and a can of soda to her lips. Elena stared out the patio window, her hand to her ear. William sat on the sofa, bent over, tying his shoe. All were frozen in eerie silence.

Bodhi adjusted the hands on the timepiece as sounds filled his eardrums like the ocean crashing against the rocks. Cassie glanced toward Bodhi and spewed ginger ale all over the counter. "Dad?"

William finished tying his shoe and stood, confused. Elena slowly turned and faced him. "Corazón? ¡Gracias a Dios!" They rushed into each other's arms. Bodhi planted a hard, wet kiss on her lips and spun her like a dance partner. She hooked her right leg around his waist and ran her fingers along his pecs.

Cassie cleared her throat and wrinkled her brow. "Seriously?" She balled up a dishcloth and tossed it at them. "Uh, guys. Save that little thing you're doing, right there, for later, please … I can't unsee that now."

Bodhi removed Gram's ring and replaced it on Elena's finger.

"This saved my life, sweetheart. Thank you."

Muffled shouting jarred him from his moment of peace.

"We gotta go. Abara wants the relics and plans on sending us into the past. He has Phillip to do his dirty work now."

A gyrating vortex exploded like sparkling jewels inside vibrant clouds of gas. Bodhi, Elena, William, and Cassie, with Baby William in her arms, leaped into the mouth of the wormhole and escaped.

SEVENTEEN

The roar of the ocean was deafening. Black waves crashed into the jagged opening of a sea cave, churning foam and spraying a salty mist into the shadows. A flash of blue light flickered like lightning inside the cavern, and in an instant, five figures tumbled onto the slick stone floor, tangled and gasping.

"Dad? Elena? Where the heck are we? William? Are you okay?"

"Your guess is as good as mine, Blondie. We're in the mouth of a cave, and by the smell of things, we need to find our way out of here."

"Fúchila … it smells like a slaughterhouse in here."

"Elena, can you take the baby while I fix my shoe?"

"Of course, Mija. Aw, come to Nana, my handsome niño."

William pointed towards the rear of the cave. "Looks like a stairway cut into the stone of that back wall."

The ancient stairway was covered in moss and faded into darkness. A faint golden glow filtered down from above, flickering and glistening. Muffled voices and soft music echoed in the night.

"That's firelight from torches. We must be below a city," Elena said.

A wave exploded inside the mouth of the cave, drenching them with an icy spray of saltwater. Cassie shrilled. Elena darted behind a rock, shielding Little William.

A distant church bell rang out, followed by cannon fire and booming cheers.

Cassie grabbed William's wrist. "You hear that? Sounds like Spanish. Like a celebration of some kind going on up there. Maybe we're in Rio?"

Elena handed the baby over to Cassie and strained to listen, her eyes narrowing. "That's colonial Spanish. The accent is centuries old."

They moved as a group towards the stone stairway. Bodhi took the lead, testing the stairs. "Watch your step. It's wet and slick."

A faint gasp echoed above them. The group froze. A local boy, no older than ten, peered down the edge of the staircase. His dark eyes widened at the glowing compass in Bodhi's right hand. He made the sign of the Cross, whispered, "demonios del mar," then bolted up the steps.

"Oye, Bodhi. Hide the Compass. This is not the place and time for miraculous objects."

"Sorry. I was using it to see where we're going."

Cassie sighed. "Ugh. That's not good."

Elena pushed past Bodhi. "Let me go first, Señor."

"I'd prefer you walk behind me, Love."

"I can handle myself, amigo, and I'm the only one who speaks Spanish."

Bodhi nodded. "Good point. You go first."

Elena kissed him on the cheek. "Wait here. I'll be right back."

"What? Where you going?" he protested.

"This is what I do. Trust me. I won't be long."

Elena disappeared up the stairs and into the darkness. Cassie tugged at his sleeve. "Where'd she go, Dad? Shouldn't you follow her?"

"Nope. This is how she rolls."

"Seriously? You're going to let your wife wander a strange city at night all by herself and—"

"She was a Union spy, Cass. An American hero. She knows what she's doing. I trust her."

Cassie heaved a quivering breath. "Heroine, Dad."

"What?"

"Heroine. Not hero."

"Nuance."

"This place makes me nervous, and the baby's getting fussy. We need to find shelter."

William tugged at her arm and handed her his jacket. "You're shivering, darling. Here. Let me take Little William."

"No, that's okay—"

"Blondie, take the coat. Have a seat behind that rock out of the breeze until Elena gets back."

Cassie frowned at Bodhi and allowed William to slip the jacket around her shoulders. William took her by the hand and guided her behind the boulder, where they huddled away from the frigid air and icy ocean spray.

Bodhi squatted on the second step of the stairway and rubbed his palms together, blowing warm air into his cupped hands. Thirty minutes later, he jerked from a poke on his shoulder.

"Look what I found. Clothes. They'll help us blend."

She dropped a woven basket full of clothing onto the wet stone floor.

"Ah ... You scared the crap out of me, girl."

"You're always so jumpy, Bodhi."

"If you'd stop sneaking up on me like somebody's cat, maybe I wouldn't be."

"I told you many times ... I have skills. Deal with it, as you say."

Elena yanked the clothing from the basket and tossed them to the group one by one. Cassie slipped on a layered, ankle-length cotton dress, colored olive and yellow, a shawl to cover her head, and leather sandals.

Elena slipped into a colorful red, blue, and green frilled dress, sandals, and a white mantilla head covering.

"Oh, wow, Elena. That's adorable. You look so *Spanish*. And I love this dress you picked out for me."

Bodhi rolled his eyes. "Can we stop with the fashion show? What's in there for me and Will?"

"Wait your turn, amigo."

She tossed a tiny cotton shirt and rope belt to Cassie. "For the baby."

Elena handed William a bundle of clothes: a pair of cotton trousers with strings at the waist, a collarless white cotton shirt, open at the neck, leather boots, and a straw hat.

Cassie giggled. "You look like a wannabe pirate, Cappie. But a sexy wannabe pirate."

"Yeah, thanks, Cass. They kind of itch."

Bodhi paced. "This isn't dress-up time, gang. What do you have for me in that basket? We need to move."

Elena pulled out several items of wardrobe and handed them to Bodhi. He slipped on a close-fitting, padded jacket with decorative gold embroidery, complete with a short black velvet cape draped over his shoulder, a flat cap with a feather plume, short padded pumpkin breeches that ballooned around his hips and thighs, white tights, and black leather shoes with buckles.

Cassie wheezed and collapsed to the ground, crying with laughter. Her giggles turned to shrills. "Oh my God, Dad. You look like King Henry the Eighth. The only thing missing is a turkey drumstick." She held her stomach and screeched. William stifled a chuckle, his face reddening as he fought back his laughter and snorted.

Elena stepped backward and raised her hands. "Oh, Mi Amore, you look so handsome as a nobleman." Her words caused Cassie and William to lose it completely.

Bodhi's neck tingled, and his face flushed. "I can't wear this. If I walk around like this, I'll get rolled by thugs. Come on, Elena, this has to be a joke, right?"

Elena's straight face finally cracked, and she burst into giggles. "Sí, Señora Bodhi. I finally played my joke on you." She shrugged and smirked. "I can be funny too…"

"Okay, ya got me. Now, where are my actual clothes?"

Elena handed him a bundle of clothes similar to William's. She cocked her head and rested her hand on her hip while he dressed. "That's muy bueno, Corazón. You weren't quite ready to be a prince."

Elena tossed Cassie a loaf of bread, a block of cheese, and a small jug of goat's milk. "The milk is for our niño."

Bodhi left a peck on Elena's cheek and asked, "Where'd you find all of this stuff?"

"I stole it."

"You stole it?"

"Sí."

"So, there's a nobleman running around town without his pumpkin pants?"

"Sí. I can return them if you like."

"No, that's okay. They might come in handy if we need a parachute at some point. What else did you learn on your shopping trip?"

"Well, we are in Colombia—the city of Cartagena. We must have arrived somewhere in the early to mid-1600s."

William gasped, "Good Lord. The Golden Age of Pirates."

Elena nodded. "Sí, this is a very dangerous place to be. Not only pirates and smugglers, but disease. Yellow fever. Malaria. And even worse, the Spanish Inquisition. I saw a man being dragged away, whispering prayers in Latin. We must not draw attention to ourselves."

"Why would the relics bring us here?" Cassie asked.

Elena glanced at Bodhi. He tightened his lips and raised his brows. "No way to know, Cass. The good news is they can't follow us, so we're safe to hide out for a while. The bad news is, we're in Cartagena, 1600 and something."

Elena gripped Bodhi's hand. "We need somewhere to hide while we figure out why we're here. Maybe there's a cave outside of town or—"

Bodhi raised his finger to his lips. "Sh."

The local boy was back. He crept along the wall of the stairway, attempting to hide in the shadows.

Elena whispered, "Puedes salir, mijo." *You can come out, son.*

The boy approached, his head lowered, but his eyes fixed on Elena.

"Cómo te llamas?" she asked. *What's your name?*

"Simón," he muttered. "Simón Hernández-López."

"¿Dónde está tu familia?" *Where's your family?*

"No tengo familia." *I have no family.*

Elena kneeled next to him and extended her arms, inviting a hug. Simón tugged on her arm.

"Sígueme. Hay peligro aquí," he said.

Elena glanced at the group. "He wants us to follow him. He says we are in danger if we stay here."

Bodhi pointed at the stairway. "Lead the way. Vámonos, as Elena would say."

Simón led them up the stairway and into the market. Massive stone walls surrounded the ancient city, thick and sunbaked, built to repel pirate sieges. The smell of limestone dust and salt hung in the air.

Narrow cobbled streets wove between whitewashed buildings with wooden balconies draped in vines and laundry. Homes were close together, but the wealthy estates were inset with heavy iron gates and courtyards. Torches illuminated the streets.

Church bells rang at odd hours, marking prayers, curfews, or executions. Baroque cathedrals rose in the center, their gold-plated altars casting long shadows.

Soldiers in red wool coats and black leather boots patrolled, muskets slung over their shoulders, keeping a close eye on the enslaved and poor. Cartagena was a bustling colonial port city—part Spanish fortress, part tropical labyrinth.

Simón pointed at Bodhi and whispered something to Elena. She turned toward Bodhi and said, "Simón wants you to keep the Compass hidden. He says the Tribunal will hang you for witchcraft if they see you with it."

Bodhi nodded. "Understood. And that goes for the timepiece and the Tempus Glass. We can't be seen with any of them."

Simón led them through the city to a hidden tunnel in the fortress wall that ran beneath the prison and the docks. He lit a torch and guided them through a labyrinth of tunnels etched in the rock that dripped with seawater and moss.

A rat scurried over Cassie's foot. She shrieked. William clamped his hand over her mouth and pulled her close. "I'm afraid we're going to encounter more of those critters, Cass. Try to ignore them."

"I hate rats. You know that. I can't …"

"You can, darling. Keep moving."

"Easy for you to say with your fancy boots. Look at my feet. I'm in sandals. I felt his hairy little toes on my ankle. Ew."

Simón pushed aside a wooden barrel and moved a couple of stone bricks. He turned toward the group and waved his hand.

They ducked inside a three-foot crawl space into a ten-by-twenty-foot room. A straw-filled mattress lay in the corner next to a crude circular wooden table with a dagger stuck in the center. Several animal skins filled with water hung over the back wall. A pile of apple cores, moldy bread, animal skeletons, and fish heads rotted inside a wooden crate. The air was musty and filled with a stench of decay and urine.

He raised his hands and grinned. "Eres bienvenido a quedarte." *You are welcome to stay.*

Elena whispered in Bodhi's ear. "He wants us to stay."

Bodhi raised an eyebrow. "Well, we don't have any better offers at the moment, so why not?"

Little William's wails echoed off the walls. Simón's eyes widened, and he quickly handed Cassie a stick, insisting she take it. "Caña de azúcar," he said.

Cassie rocked the baby and glanced at Elena.

"It's sugar cane, Mija."

Little William's wails were quickly replaced with suckling noises and coos. Simón slid the torch into a rusted sconce, casting a warm, flickering glow across the stone walls.

"Let's rest here tonight and look for a five-star hotel in the morning."

"Real funny, Dad."

Elena tapped Cassie on the shoulder. "Simón wants you and the baby to sleep on the mattress."

"Aw, what a sweet gesture." She gazed at Simón and nodded. "Muchas gracias, Simón," she said in her limited Spanish and clumsy American accent.

Bodhi laid out the King Henry outfit against the wall and motioned for Elena to join him. "I told you this thing would be useful." She laid her head on his chest and closed her eyes.

William spooned Cassie and the baby, and the soft snores of the night began like a coordinated nocturnal orchestra. Elena's deep sighs caused Bodhi's head to bob until they finally lulled him into a deep sleep.

Simón lay down next to Elena and curled into a fetal position. She wrapped her arm around his waist.

"Buenas noches, mijo," she said as she caressed his forehead.

Bodhi jerked. His eyes popped open to complete darkness. The left side of his body was numb beneath Elena, and something in the air was amiss. How long had he slept? Soft breaths were the only sounds, each with its own rhythm. One sound seemed to be missing. He reached for Simón, but he wasn't there.

"Elena," he whispered. "Wake up."

"Huy, Bodhi ... let me sleep."

"Where's Simón?"

"He's right—"

"No. He's not."

"I can't see Cariño. It's as dark as pitch in here."

"Exactly. The torch burned out ... or it's gone."

"Use the light from the Compass."

He shuffled through his pockets, patting himself down.

"It's gone. Elena, the Compass is gone. Shit."

"It can't be. Check again."

"What do you mean, it can't be? It's gone. And that little street rat stole it and left us in the dark."

"You don't know that, Bodhi." Elena slipped the Tempus Glass from her pocket and hummed. A soft emerald glow filled the cavern as the green sands stirred.

The torch was missing from the sconce on the wall, and Simón was nowhere in sight.

"The kid's a thief, Elena. Thank God he didn't swipe the Tempus Glass," Bodhi grumbled.

146

"He only knew of *your* relic, Bodhi … not mine, or Cassie's.

So, what are you saying?

"I'm not saying anything."

"I think you are. It's my fault—"

"No. Of course not … Well, if you had kept it hidden like Cassie and me …"

"It's definitely my fault."

"Bodhi, we can trace the location of the Compass and recover it."

"That's true. Hopefully, he doesn't accidentally figure out how to use it."

"He'd have to be a *sensitive*, Bodhi. I doubt he is. He's probably trying to pawn it for his next meal."

Elena chanted and closed her eyes. The Tempus Glass revealed an image of a room full of men drinking rum and playing games. Pirates. Smugglers.

"The Compass isn't far, Bodhi. Let's go get it back."

"Should I wake Cassie and Will?"

"Let them sleep. We'll be back before they wake."

Elena led the way out of the tunnels to the streets and quickly hid the light of the hourglass.

"This way. Inside there."

They slipped through the door of a dank and dim tavern filled with cigar smoke, body odor, and the scent of stale lavender. Three men in the corner tossed dice on a board with three horizontal lines and twelve spaces, grumbling and tossing coin bets. Two other men arm wrestled in another corner while onlookers placed bets and shouted.

A bartender emerged behind the counter and asked what they wanted to drink.

"Dos rones por favor," Elena responded.

"Oh, Bodhi, we haven't drunk rum together in so long."

"Uh, stay focused, Chica. We're not here to drink and party."

Elena slammed her shot, closing her eyes, relishing every drop. "Muy bueno." She grinned at the bartender and raised two fingers.

She slammed the next one and pushed the other shot toward Bodhi.

"Elena. Focus," he whispered as he downed the shot.

"Huy, you're no fun. Where's that big, strong hombre I fell in love with, huh?"

"Trying to save our asses."

Simón entered the bar from another room. His eyes widened when he spotted Bodhi and Elena. Bodhi pointed. "There he is."

Simón ducked behind a pirate and whispered something in his ear. The smuggler turned and rose from his chair, his hand resting on a large flint-lock pistol. He approached the bar, chuckling and chewing on a stogie.

Bodhi rose to meet him, but Elena cut in front of him, planting her fists firmly on her hips.

The pirate sneered and spat the stogie at her feet. "¿Qué quieres con el chico?" *What do you want with the boy?*

Elena narrowed her eyes. "Él tomó algo que me pertenece." *He took something that belongs to me.*

The pirate reached into his pocket and removed the Compass. He nodded and snickered. "Ofréceme algo mejor." *Offer me something better.*

Elena removed the Tempus Glass and chanted. The sands stirred and glowed. The pirate took two steps backward and grunted. In an instant, time froze. Bodhi snatched the Compass from the pirate's hand and quickly stuffed it in his pocket.

"Let's go, Elena."

"Wait. One momento." She snagged the bottle of rum from the bar and swigged. "Let's get drunk, Bodhi."

He chuckled. Her allure and seductive tone were too much. "Well, since we have nothing but time on our hands at the moment, I know a sweet spot by the ocean."

They sat on a rock with their feet in the cool water, taking turns swigging sips of rum. Elena giggled, nibbling on his earlobe and running her fingers along his pecs. She whispered, "Have your way with me, Cariño. Right here by the sea."

Bodhi swooped her in his arms and set her knee-deep in the water, slipping her dress off her shoulders, exposing her raw beauty beneath the soft blue moonlight. Elena tossed their clothes onto the beach. The couple dipped beneath the waves and made passionate love under the stars. Time literally stood still, then resumed without them realizing it.

They lay side-by-side on the beach, half-dressed as a crimson sun crested in the distance. A mob approached, led by a priest from the Tribunal.

"She's a witch," a woman shouted in Spanish. "They are fornicators! Hang them!" she continued.

Bodhi and Elena scrambled to slip their clothes on and gather the relics, as the mob overpowered them, confiscating the relics.

"These are the talismans they worship the Devil with," the priest shouted. "Seize them! They will face the wrath of the Tribunal for their evil deeds this day."

EIGHTEEN

They led Bodhi and Elena to a hall inside a Baroque-style building under construction. Their hands were bound by rope as a growing crowd jeered them with insults and spat on them.

They forced them to their knees in front of an altar where the priest loomed over them and two Spanish soldiers flanked them on either side. A table to their left seated half a dozen priests and noblemen.

The priest raised a bible and addressed the room in Spanish, pointing at the Mariner's Compass and the Tempus Glass. "The accused were witnessed performing magic with these talismans, serving the Devil, and they are guilty of fornication in a public place. Judgment, in this case, will be swift and just. They are guilty and will hang by the neck until dead at noon today. May God have mercy on their souls."

The priest waved his hand toward the soldiers. "Take them away."

Bodhi whispered, "What did he say?"

"We're guilty of loving each other, and we're to be hanged at noon."

"Great. Just when I thought our day couldn't get any worse."

A soldier cut their bindings, and as the ropes tumbled to the floor, they shoved them into a dank, dark prison cell. Echoes clamored a final warning as the iron door slammed shut. The stone walls glistened in the flickering torchlight and radiated a deathly chill. The air was heavy and dark with the suffering souls of those who came before them.

Bodhi collected straw from the floor and gathered Elena into his arms. She shivered and laid her head on his chest.

"Is this the end, Mi Amore?"

"No, sweetheart. It's not. We'll figure this out."

"We only have hours, Bodhi…"

"I'm concentrating on the timepiece … hoping Cassie can—"

Stone scraped across the floor opposite them. They jerked and retreated into the shadows.

"What the heck?" Bodhi tiptoed toward the sound, squinting, searching the dark.

A two-foot square stone vibrated, pushing dust and sand into the cell. Bodhi gripped the corners of the stone and pulled. A small, shadowy figure climbed over the stone and darted into the cell.

"Por aquí. Rápido." *This way. Quickly.*

"Simón?" Elena whispered.

"Sí. Sígueme," he insisted.

"Bodhi, he wants us to follow him. It's a way out."

"And we trust this little thief?"

"We have no choice. ¡Vamos!"

Bodhi pushed the stone back into place as they entered a small passageway and whispered, "They're really going to think we're witches now with this Houdini act."

Simón led them through a labyrinth of tunnels back to his hidden lair. As they slipped inside the room, Cassie greeted them with a broad smile.

"Where've you guys been all morning? We were just getting ready to come looking for you. Did you find anywhere nice to eat? We're starving."

Cassie looked them up and down and frowned. "Wait. What happened to your clothes?"

William tapped Cassie on the shoulder. "Darling, by the looks on their faces, I don't think they were eating breakfast or sightseeing."

Cassie's eyes widened. "Did something happen? What am I missing?"

Bodhi heaved a breath and shook his head. "It's a long story, Cass. We need the timepiece."

"Oh, my God. Why? What's going on, Dad?"

"Let's just say the Catholic Church thinks we're witches and took possession of our relics. We need the timepiece to get them back."

"Seriously? How'd you guys manage that?"

"It doesn't matter. Let's go get the relics and get the hell out of here before something worse happens."

Elena kneeled next to Simón and spoke to him in Spanish. "Why, Mijo? Why would you steal from us?"

Simón shrugged, his glistening eyes the size of orbs. "I was curious … I only wanted to see the magic. Then they stole it from me."

"Who?"

"The smugglers. I followed them to the tavern to steal it back, but that's when you walked in. I'm very sorry."

"It's okay, Mijo. We forgive you. Thank you for rescuing us from the prison."

He nodded and lowered his head. Elena pulled him to her breast and hugged him.

"Why are you hugging him? He's the reason we're in this mess."

"He was trying to steal the Compass back from the smugglers, Bodhi. It's not his fault. He made a mistake. He was curious."

"Well, curiosity killed the cat. And almost got us killed." Bodhi scowled at Simón. He tucked himself behind Elena.

Cassie handed Bodhi the timepiece. "Be nice, Dad. He's just a little boy."

Bodhi glared at Simón and pointed at the timepiece. "Muy peligroso. Very dangerous."

The group shadowed Simón through the tunnels and back to the main street. He led them to the doorstep of the building where their death sentence awaited.

"Will, you and Cassie wait here while Elena and I retrieve the relics. And try to stay out of sight."

Bodhi and Elena approached the entrance, met by a Spanish soldier drawing his sword. Bodhi adjusted the hands of the timepiece and mumbled. The soldier took a step towards them and froze mid-stride.

They scurried through a grand hallway into the room where they had been dragged before the altar earlier. The Inquisition Tribunal sat frozen. A poor soul knelt, beaten and in chains, before the priest. An elderly woman with long, frayed gray hair, dressed in rags and a tall conical hat on her head.

"This is disgusting, Bodhi. How could they do this to innocent people? To this poor woman. She's someone's abuela."

"The reason they called it the *Dark Ages*, babe. Why is she wearing a dunce hat?"

"It's a coroza—a symbol of her supposed crime. It's not right." Elena snatched a set of keys from one of the soldiers and removed the old woman's chains.

"What are you doing? They're going to think she's a witch for sure if they see she escaped from her chains."

"We're rescuing her, Bodhi. I'll grab the relics. You carry this poor woman out of here. She looks like my nana Greta."

"And you say *I* want to save everyone? Grab the relics. I've got Nana."

"One more thing before we go, Bodhi."

"Oh, man. What are you up to now?"

Elena removed the priest's robes and bound his wrists with the chains. She placed the coroza atop his head and nodded. "There. Now the real criminal is where he belongs."

Bodhi chuckled. "He's going to have a hell of a time explaining his way out of that." He lifted the old woman over his shoulder and glanced at Elena. "Let's go, before you get any more bright ideas."

"Wait." The Tempus Glass glowed in her hands. She gazed into its stirring sands.

"Come on, Elena. Let's go. Pronto."

Outside the building, Bodhi set the old woman gently on the ground. He moved the hands of the timepiece, and the world around them resumed.

The woman's eyes blinked rapidly, glancing at the family surrounding her, trying to speak, but her words would not reach her lips.

Elena took her hand and squeezed. "You're safe now, Señora," she said in Spanish. She pointed at Simón. "This poor boy is an orphan. He needs a family. God has spared your life today. He asks you to take this little boy as your own and care for him."

Tears gushed over the woman's cheeks. Her arms opened to Simón, and she whispered in his ear.

Elena kissed Simón on top of his head and hugged him. "Go with her. She's your family now. Hurry, before the soldiers come."

Simón led the woman by the hand into the streets, where they disappeared into the bustling crowds and busy markets.

Cassie dabbed her eyes. "That was so beautiful. We saved them, Elena." She placed her hand over her heart and turned toward Bodhi. "Dad, wasn't that awesome?"

"The boy will save many lives from the Inquisition and become a great leader in the community. The woman will see to it. This was their destiny," Elena said.

"How do you know this?" Cassie asked.

The Tempus Glass revealed it to me when I took it away from the Tribunal. The woman is the mother of a powerful nobleman. Simón Hernández-López is my ancestor, and the reason we're here. To ensure the boy's safety by fixing an altered timeline before it could jeopardize mine."

"That might explain his urge to steal things," Bodhi mumbled.

Elena smacked his arm and chuckled. "Not funny. I only steal when our lives depend on it. It's called surviving."

Shouts echoed through the streets coming from the direction of the Inquisition building.

"We need to go. Like, right now," Bodhi warned.

They held hands and sang. A whirlwind stirred, kicking up dust and ripping open a massive vortex in space and time.

NINETEEN

They tumbled onto a soft, burnt-red desert floor etched by warm breezes, surrounded by acacia trees, wild grasses, and brush adorned with vibrant desert flowers. The air was a blend of pungent, earthy scents: eucalyptus, dry sand, and a hint of garlic. Clicks of insects, whistling winds, and the random chirps of wrens surrounded them. In the distance, ancient rock formations rose above the desert like massive red domes.

A hundred yards south was an oasis of yellow buildings, their roofs lined with solar panels, reflecting the glaring sunlight. Enormous trees encircled the buildings like guardians, and the warmth of a sturdy rustic lodge seemed to invite them.

Elena rested one hand on her hip and shielded her eyes with the other, scanning the landscape. "Where is this place, Bodhi? Where have you taken us?"

"We're Down Under, my love." He pointed toward the oasis. "I say we head to that lodge and check things out."

William chuckled. "Well, you said Australia was your vacation of choice, Bodhi. The relics must have heard you."

"Dad? Um, don't you think we'll look a bit odd walking into that lodge? ... Ya know, like, seventeenth century odd?"

"Not much of a choice, Blondie. Wherever we are, hopefully, my credit card hasn't expired."

Bodhi pushed through the door and peered inside. A young man with sunbaked skin, sandy blonde hair, and smiling green eyes glanced up from behind the counter, beaming. Bodhi stepped inside the lobby as the group shuffled in behind him.

"G'day, mate. Looks like ya wandered in from the bush," he chuckled. "Look'n for a room or two, yeah? By the looks of ya, maybe some clothes?"

Bodhi nodded and placed both palms on the counter. "Two rooms will do. And—"

Elena interrupted. "We're coming from a costume ball, and our luggage was stolen."

"Stolen, you say?"

Cassie wrinkled her brow and glanced at Bodhi, then at the clerk, who grinned back at her. "You're Americans … welcome."

Elena lifted a newspaper from a coffee table near a water cooler. She flashed the paper at Bodhi and whispered, "We're in the present time."

She ran her index finger across the heading and tapped the date.

September 20, 2038

Bodhi smiled, removed his leather wallet, and snapped an American Express on the counter.

The clerk lifted the card and squinted to read it. "Well, at least the crooks didn't snatch your wallet, eh?"

The clerk slid two keys across the counter and winked. "All set, folks. Should I contact the cops for ya? To report your luggage stolen?"

Bodhi shook his head. "Not necessary."

The clerk smacked the counter and nodded. "Right then. Pleasant day. Let me know if ya need anything else."

Elena and Cassie spent the next two hours buying clothes and baby food at a local market. They returned to the lodge with an armload of shopping bags and paused in the hallway in front of their rooms.

Cassie set her bags on the floor, hugged Elena, and swung her door open. "I'm going to give the baby a bath and take a shower. Give William a break. Let's all get together for dinner later. I'll find us a nice, fun place to eat, and we can have a few drinks."

"Oh, that sounds muy bueno, Mija. I need a short siesta myself. My feet are throbbing and my head is pounding."

Elena opened the door to find Bodhi snoring, spread-eagled across a queen-sized bed, and naked as a newborn. She allowed her clothes to drop to the floor and cuddled up next to him, grabbing his wrist and forcing his arm around her. She smiled contentedly, snuggling into the warmth of his body and drifting off to sleep.

Bodhi and his family gathered around a table on the patio of the *Little Wallaby Steakhouse and Bar,* a half a mile from their lodge. Bodhi couldn't keep his eyes off Elena, and William caressed and kissed Cassie's hand, constantly whispering in her ear. Little William drummed his highchair with a plastic spoon between slurps of a koala bear sippy cup.

"Dad? Hello." She waved her hand in front of his face. "Eyes over here, buddy. Maybe take a picture. It'll last longer."

Bodhi shook his head. "Yeah, sorry. I'm a bit mesmerized."

"I know, right? Doesn't she look absolutely stunning? I helped her pick that dress out. She looks like Penélope Cruz, only taller. Prettier."

"Ay ay ay, you all are embarrassing me. Look at *you,* Mija. You're gorgeous. And Bodhi and William. Such handsome hombres." She pointed at Little William. "And you too, Mijo." She puckered her lips and baby-talked. "My handsome little Sancho."

Bodhi tapped his wineglass with his spoon. "Well, now that we've established how beautiful we all are, I have some things I want to talk about with my family."

Cassie scowled. "Oh no. What now, Dad? Please tell me this is good news and not something you forgot to tell us."

Elena grasped his hand and gazed deeply into his eyes, her eyebrows rising to a peak.

"I have some important things to share. But first, can we raise our glasses and toast our family? You're the reason I get out of bed each morning. God has blessed me with each one of you."

His eyes grew misty as he raised his glass. "To you, my beautiful family, whom I love more than life. Thank you for always being there for me. Cheers."

Cassie raised her glass. Her eyes widened with concern. "Cheers, Daddy."

William raised his glass and nodded. Elena tapped her glass to Bodhi's and smiled. "Salut, Mi Amore."

Little William giggled, banged his cup on the high chair, and launched it across the table. Bodhi's eyes followed the path of the cup—a beaming grin forming across his lips.

"The kid's got an arm … I'm telling ya…"

Elena patted Bodhi's wrist. "Say what you need to say, Cariño. We're listening."

Bodhi heaved a breath and downed his entire glass of wine.

"Whoa, Dad. Ya might want to pump the brakes on that vino, dude."

He chuckled and wiped a tear before it revealed itself. "We're not in Australia by accident."

Cassie and William glanced at each other, then gazed at Bodhi. Elena raised an eyebrow and tilted her head. "What do you mean?"

"Before I traveled back to 2012 to close the black hole, I spent days studying and memorizing the Tome of Cassiel … to learn how to return the relics to him."

"Is that why we're in Australia, Bodhi?" William asked.

"Yes … and no. We're here because I wanted to spend the vacation of a lifetime with you. Do fun stuff and crazy things as a family and visit a place we've never seen."

Cassie shrugged and cocked her head. "Well, you definitely nailed that one, Dad."

"I've set up a jeep tour, a guided Mala Walk with an Aboriginal ranger, a little river cruise to spot crocodiles…"

Cassie frowned. "Uh, no, Dad. No crocodiles for me, thank you very much."

"Me either, Bodhi. Huy, are you loco? Crocodiles?"

"Alright, Will and I will go. You up for it, Will?"

"I'm all in, Bodhi. A trip for the fellas will be a swell adventure."

He pulled the baby from his high chair and raised him in the air. "Crocodiles, little fella…"

Cassie snatched him away, holding him to her breast, frowning at William.

"Don't even think about it," she whispered.

Bodhi continued. "Great. The point is, I felt we needed this vacation and time to bond as a family and create an experience together, doing something fun instead of always being on the run."

Elena narrowed her eyes and crossed her arms, leaning back in her seat. "And what is the 'Yes' part, Bodhi?"

"What do you mean?"

"The 'Yes'. What is the other reason we're here?"

"Uluru."

"Ay, and what is that? What's Uluru?"

"It's a sacred monolith." He pointed out the window. "See that giant red mound over there? That's Uluru."

The server and several helpers began setting plates of food around the table. Bodhi laid his napkin on his lap and glanced at Elena, fidgeting in her seat. She opened her mouth to speak but hesitated until the servers were gone.

Bodhi nodded. "The blessing, Elena."

She nibbled on her lower lip and sighed. With her hands folded on the table, she spoke a blessing over the meal and her family and made the sign of the Cross.

Elena twisted her body toward Bodhi and glared. "Go on. You were saying…"

"What I was saying is, Uluru is a sacred rock formation to the Anangu people, the traditional owners of the land. It is considered a significant site in their culture. They believe ancestral beings created Uluru during the Dreamtime."

"What is this Dreamtime, Bodhi?" Elena asked as she cut into her steak.

"It's the period when the land and its features were formed. The Anangu have a deep spiritual connection to Uluru and believe that ancestral spirits still live within it."

"Where did you learn of this? The tome?"

"Yep."

"Huy, Bodhi, so what is the significance of all of this? Get to the point, my brain is starting to hurt."

"Yeah, Dad, get to the point. What does all of this mean?"

"According to the tome, many years ago, the elder of the Anangu people wandered into a sacred and forbidden area of Uluru and discovered the relics in their celestial form. They were once orbs. One emerald, one violet, and one golden. They were left unattended on a dais—an altar. Seeing no one was around, the Elder stole the relics and hid them in his village, where he experimented with them."

"Ay dios mío." Elena covered her mouth with her palm.

"Holy crap, Dad. So, what happened?"

"Removal of the relics from the altar caused them to shift from the heavenly realm into the physical world as ordinary objects: a timepiece, a mariner's compass, and an hourglass—Their power hidden within."

Cassie dabbed her lips with her napkin. "I'm feeling nauseous. I hate to ask, but where is this story leading?"

"The tome instructs a 'Son of Humanity' to return the relics to the dais in the forbidden location where they were stolen. There, the angel Cassiel will reclaim them."

Cassie bit her lip and grimaced. "And is that person *you*, Dad?"

"Yes, Blondie. I traced a copy of the map to the sacred location from the tome. When our vacation ends, I'll travel to Uluru and return the relics to Cassiel."

Cass shook her head. "This is so unbelievable. Why does it have to be you, Dad?"

"Because I'm the only one who understands what needs to be done. I know the prayer and the location of the sacred site."

"And what happens to you after you return them?"

"Let's finish our vacation first, Cass. Then I'll explain the rest. Can you grant me that?"

Cassie tossed her napkin on the table and scooched her chair out. She darted around the table and hugged his neck. "Of course we can, Daddy. I love you so much, and I'm so scared right now."

He hugged her back and kissed her cheek. "You don't have to be scared, Blondie. I promise everything will be okay."

Elena squeezed Bodhi's hand and raised her glass. "Let's give another toast to your papa, Cassie, and enjoy the rest of our dinner." She pointed to the orange sunset out the window. "Cheers to this beautiful setting. Tonight, we dance, we drink, and make passionate love." Elena rubbed Bodhi's thigh and gazed at him.

Cassie shielded herself with her palm. "Ugh. A little too much information, if you know what I mean. How 'bout we stick to dancing and drinking for now, hm?"

TWENTY

Bodhi squinted, opening one eye to the soft rays of golden sunlight beaming through their curtains. His head pounded, and his throat was dry. He yawned and stretched his body, accidentally pulling the sheet away from Elena, exposing her. He gazed at the curvaceous contours of her body as she slept, gently running his fingers over the curves of her strong jawline—the jawline of a proud and elegant woman. His heart ached. The depth of his passion for her was like a hidden chasm of dark, still waters. He was smitten and bewitched by her charms years ago and fell hopelessly in love with her as their time together slowly passed. How could he ever live without her now? The thought of breaking her heart would be soul-crushing.

She whimpered and tugged at the sheets in protest, pulling them over her head. He joined her beneath the sheets, caressing her thighs and brushing his lips across the nape of her neck. She shivered, her lips parting and forming a soft, crooked smile as her eyes remained closed.

"Oh, Mi Amore, you were a stallion last night. I don't know if I can satisfy your hunger again this morning. I'm drained of my essence," she whispered, resting the back of her hand on her forehead and feigning wooziness.

He cradled her face, softly kissing her cheeks and forehead, sliding toward her lips. "I'm wrecked by you, Elena. I ache for your touch, lose myself in your scent, and every time I see you, it steals the air from my lungs. I'm a hopeless mess when you're near me."

Her glistening eyes widened, and her brows rose to a soft peak. "Oh, the words you speak to my heart, my husband. They rouse something deep in my soul. Something I've never known with any man. Why am I so weak in your arms?" She kissed him with a feverish passion, tossing the sheets from the bed and climbing atop him as tears gushed down her cheeks.

"Never leave me, Corazón. You are my heart … my soul, and I will love you forever—kiss you with my dying breath. Make love to me, Mi Amore. Ravish me again and again until I collapse in your arms like a helpless kitten."

Bodhi and Elena sat on a wooden bench outside the lodge, waiting for Cassie and Will. They locked arms, their fingers intertwined, Elena resting her head on his shoulder. She sighed and whispered. "What's going to happen, Cariño? My heart is terrified for you. For us."

"It'll be okay, love. I'll finish this, and you and I will die in our bed old and gray and a hundred and ten years old."

"I pray to the Virgin that this is so … Bodhi, I've been having nightmares."

"What kind of nightmares?"

"I race through a dark maze, searching for you, but I can never find you. I hear your voice, but something or someone takes you away from me. I wake up only to find I am still dreaming, sitting in front of the graves of my sons, Santiago and Gabriel. When I finally awaken, I'm soaked in sweat and tears, and my heart is shattered."

"I'll never leave you, sweetheart. I'll always find you … no matter how dark or hopeless the situation. Always remember that."

She sniffled and kissed his cheek. The shuffling of feet drew their attention towards the lodge entrance.

"Oh my God, Dad, you look like Crocodile Dundee." She shrilled.

"Uh, thanks, Cass. I kind of like my fit."

He modeled his camo shorts, rust-colored short-sleeved shirt, tan felt fedora, and hiking boots like a pro.

"We went shopping this morning, Mija. Your papa needed shorts and a hat. Good thing because the sun is strong this morning. Isn't he so handsome?"

"Well, you look adorable, Elena. Love the sunglasses. So, boujee."

William patted Bodhi's shoulder. "You look like a cool cat, sport."

"Thanks, Will. At least someone appreciates style."

Cassie giggled and kissed his cheek. "I'm teasing, Daddy. You look amazing. Love the kangaroo backpack by the way." She winked and clicked her tongue.

"It was all they had, Blondie. We needed something to put water bottles and bug spray in."

"No, seriously, it's cute on you," she giggled. "So, where are you taking us?"

"Today, we do the guided Mala Walk with the Aboriginal rangers. We'll get an up-close look at Uluru and experience a little of the Outback. Sooo, … if you're ready, let's roll."

Bodhi led the way, holding Elena's hand, followed by William with the baby tucked into a carrier strapped to his back. Cassie trailed, stumbling, and smearing sunscreen over the baby's legs, arms, and face.

After the ranger briefing and Q&A, the family headed up the road—a three-foot-wide trail roped off on either side. They crossed small bridges and strolled through the scenery of thick acacia trees and dense brush. The red walls of Uluru towered over them, parts of the walls soaked with an overflow that dripped into ponds filled with croaking frogs.

The air was dry, warm, and filled with a cacophony of scents: sage, stagnant water, and sweet, earthy aromas.

When they reached the red walls filled with ancient glyphs, Bodhi split from the group, drawn to a particular set of images: The figure of a native holding a spear gazed up at a gigantic figure holding three spirals that appeared to be radiating light.

A tap on his shoulder startled him. "What are you looking at, Bodhi?"

"These glyphs. They seem to resemble images from the tome."

"Venga, Bodhi. Can we focus on our vacation this morning? I don't want to think about tomes, maps, or relics. It's so beautiful out here, and aside from the bugs, the weather is perfecto. Let's enjoy the day, Mi Amore." She closed her eyes and filled her lungs.

He tucked the map away and kissed her lips. "Yes, my love. You're right. Let's enjoy the day." He pulled her body close.

Elena stared deep into his eyes and brushed his cheek. Emotion flooded her heart. She hugged his neck and pressed her cheek to his chest. The warmth of her tears touched his skin.

"What's the matter, sweetheart?"

"I-I don't know. My heart is so full of love for you, and I have this horrible feeling inside my chest."

He cradled her jaw. "Look at me, babe. I promise I'll keep you safe and everything will be okay."

She wiped her tears with her palms and sniffled, half laughing and half whimpering. "It isn't me I'm worried about."

Cassie's voice interrupted their moment. "Guys? The group is on the move. Let's go."

"Coming, Blondie. Right behind you."

They finished the tour, returned to the lodge, and had a light lunch. Elena fell asleep on the couch to a black and white movie. Bodhi draped a blanket over her, gently tucking it beneath her chin, while kissing the crown of her head. He slipped out of the room and tapped on Cassie's door.

"What's up, Dad? You guys have an awesome time today?"

"We did. Can we go for a walk, Blondie?"

"Uh … sure. Okay. Let me tell, William."

Bodhi took Cassie by the hand as they strolled through a small botanical garden just outside the lodge.

"Is something wrong, Daddy? Why do you look so sad?"

"Cass, promise me if anything happens to me, you'll take care of Elena."

"Oh, my God. Of course, we would … but nothing's going to happen to you, right?"

"I don't anticipate anything happening. But you never know, Cass."

"Is there something you need to tell me about Uluru? Anything I need to know? Dad? I can handle the truth."

"No, Cass. I know what I'm doing, and I'll take care of things. I just wanted to spend some alone time with you and tell you how much I love you, sweetheart."

"Dad, you're acting like a weirdo, and you're scaring me. Promise me everything is okay."

He wrapped his arm around her shoulders and hugged her, squeezing a grunt out of her. "I promise, Blondie. I'll always be here for you."

"Good. I'm going to hold you to that."

"Cass, I'd like you and Elena to go with me to Ulu<u>r</u>u in a few days. Can you ask Will to stay and take care of my grandson? I'd deeply appreciate it."

"Sure. I can arrange that. You know I'll go with you, Dad."

"Thank you. Let's head back and figure out what to eat for dinner later. Shall we?"

He gripped her hand as they wandered back to their rooms. A lump filled his throat, and a knot twisted his insides as he watched her disappear into her room.

Bodhi inhaled a shudder as he lurched upright in bed, his heart racing. The night was dark. A dry, warm breeze wafted through a partially opened window, filling the room with the sweet, earthy scent of the desert.

Elena's breaths were soft and steady, keeping her in a peaceful state of slumber. He brushed several strands of hair from her face and gently kissed her lips. She stirred and rolled over, pulling the sheet over her shoulders.

He slid the patio door open and gazed into the darkness and the pinpricks of a trillion sparkling stars above. Emotions swamped him, collapsing him into a padded chair, burying his face inside his hands.

Was it just a dream or a vision? Did he witness an unspeakable future, or was his mind playing cruel games? The low thrum and musical whispers of the relics penetrated the stillness, the vibrations unsettling his nerves. *Why are they active at this hour?*

He closed his eyes and rubbed his temples as his mind processed the visions, searching for answers or, at the very least, a logical explanation.

Bodhi witnessed the end of the world. A biblical apocalypse. A weapon of mass destruction so terrible that all life on Earth, down to the molecular level, was annihilated in seconds, leaving Earth a dead and sterile rock.

His mind was a whirlwind of thoughts and fears. What if he fails tomorrow? What if the relics fall into the wrong hands once again? He's seen the future, unless he can stop it.

A soft pair of hands massaged his shoulders. A warm, wet kiss raised the hairs on his neck. "What are you doing out here, Corazón?"

She slid next to him, tucking her arm around his waist and laying her head on his shoulder.

"Maybe you're right, Elena. What if we keep the relics hidden away? Use them for the greater good…"

"Guau, hombre. Are we even capable of such a responsibility? We would forever be on the run, and when we die, the relics would remain in the world for someone else to possess."

"We could hide them away where no one can find them."

She took his hand and kissed his knuckles. "What's troubling your heart, Mi Amore? Why are your eyes filled with so much sadness?"

His eyes glistened in the dark as he turned to face her. "I'm afraid, Elena. For the first time in my life, I'm terrified."

"What are you afraid of, husband?"

"Of failing. Losing you … losing Cass. Losing everything."

"Then let me do this, Bodhi. Let me bear this burden for us."

"No, sweetheart. I could never allow that. And it's not that simple. I've studied the tome, and I'm the only one who understands its deepest truths and most profound secrets. One mistake could be catastrophic. It's something I have to do, but …"

"But what?"

"What if, when the moment comes, I can't do it?"

"I've never known you to fail at anything, Bodhi McMullin. And I know in my heart you won't fail at this. I watched your game of football. The one you forced me to watch, and I pretended to be annoyed. But what I saw in your movie was a warrior on a battlefield, Bodhi. A man who never quit and refused to go down without a fight. The miracles I witnessed you perform were inspiring. I believe in you. Cassie believes in you. And you made me a promise."

"You've never told me that."

"I didn't want you to think I liked football. Because I don't."

"Ah, I see."

"You'll do the right thing, Bodhi. I know you. I know your heart."

"That's what scares me the most. You don't understand."

"What don't I understand, Cariño? Tell me. Help me understand."

"I have to leave you. You and Cassie. It's the price I must pay to save the world from an unimaginable apocalypse. Otherwise, these relics will fall into the wrong hands and rain down hellfire on the world."

"What do you mean? Are you talking about the warning in the scroll? Cassiel's fate?"

"Yes," he whispered.

"No. Then, you can't do this, Bodhi. We have to find another way."

"There's no other way. I've gone through every possible outcome, and only one saves our future. I have to bear this burden. No one else can."

"I can't lose you again, Corazón. I can't. I'll lie down and die."

"I've seen the future, Elena. I don't know how, but the relics have shown me what will happen if I fail."

"What will happen? What will happen, Bodhi?"

"War. A war to end all wars. A literal Armageddon. Whoever possesses the Trinity of relics will create a weapon so powerful that it will end all life on Earth in less than a second."

Elena gasped and made the sign of the Cross. "Saints have mercy on us."

Bodhi knelt in front of her, kissing her hands, the muscles in his jaw tightening. "I need you there with me, or I won't have the courage to go through with it. We must finish it, Elena. Somehow…"

He rested his head on her lap and heaved a deep, ragged breath. She ran her fingers gently through his hair, blessing him with her tears.

"Of course, I'll go with you. I would follow you through the gates of hell and back. Take me back to bed, Mi Amore, and hold me in your arms until the sunrise."

TWENTY-ONE

Uluru weighed on him. He gazed from his window at the colossal monolith looming across a red sea of sand as he sipped a black cup of coffee and nibbled on a greasy sausage roll. His stomach wouldn't let him finish the roll, so he tossed it in the garbage and washed his hands. He'd been awake since 5:00 a.m., stuffing his backpack with water, sunblock for Cassie, a miniature first aid kit, rope, hammer, stakes, and the three relics.

Elena sat up and scooched to the edge of the bed, stretching her arm in the air, arching her back, and yawning. She glanced at him, her hair disheveled and her eyes swollen from sleep, yet radiant. "Why didn't you wake me? How long have you been up?"

"Since five. I couldn't sleep, and I didn't want to disturb you. You were snoring so peacefully."

"Oye, I don't snore."

"You do, but it's cute."

She tossed a pillow at him and stepped into the shower. After weaving her hair into a tight, thick braid, she slipped into loose jeans, a T-shirt, hiking boots, and a ball cap. She pushed her sunglasses against the bridge of her nose and flashed a half-hearted smile. "I'm ready."

He tossed her a sausage roll and handed her a Styrofoam cup of steaming coffee. Bodhi slid his arms through the straps of his backpack, rolled his shoulders, and flipped his UCLA ball cap backwards. "It's now or never. Let's see if Cassie's ready."

Cassie glanced at them across the hallway as she shut her door. "Everyone's asleep. Can I put my water in your cute little kangaroo backpack, Dad?"

He rolled his eyes and turned around to grant her access. Outside, a jeep idled, waiting to take them to Uluru. Bodhi sat between Elena and Cassie with his arms around their shoulders. The closer Uluru got, the tighter he squeezed.

"Where's your Crocodile Dundee hat this morning, Pops?"

Bodhi pointed at his ball cap like a salute and raised a discerning eyebrow. "Lucky Bruins hat, Blondie. You know this already."

"You need a new one, Dad. Seriously."

Bodhi led the way up the trail back to the area of the hieroglyphs. Elena and Cassie chit-chatted for the entire walk. Bodhi kept silent, listening to the angelic sound of their voices, glancing at the map, and scouring the area for landmarks.

"Where are you leading us, Bodhi?"

"Well, according to the map, the entrance to the sacred grounds is near a place called 'The Smiling Rock'. Not sure what that means, but…"

"No smiling rocks here, Dad. Just two smiling babes. We should keep walking."

They wandered around the walls of red sandstone for nearly two hours before rounding an obscure corner and entering a cove where they discovered a large mound that looked like someone had sliced the center of a large loaf of bread with a knife, causing a split.

Cassie pointed. "If that rock's not smiling, I don't know what we're looking for."

Bodhi chuckled. "Kinda looks like Jabba the Hut without the eyes."

"Where now, Bodhi?" Elena asked, dabbing her brow with a scarf.

He pointed. "See those holes in the rock to the right of the mouth?

"Sí, Señor … but we're not going to—"

"We are."

"Oye, I was afraid you were going to say that."

Cassie rested her hands on her hips and gazed up at the side of the rock. "Wow. That's steep. Who's going first?"

"I'll go first. When I reach the top, I'll drop a rope. You ladies can decide from there who goes next."

Bodhi scaled the rock, slithered on his belly, and pulled himself over the last step to reach the top of the mound. He sat with his head between his legs, sucking breaths, and wiping the sting of salt from his eyes.

Elena hollered. "What are you doing up there, Bodhi?"

Five seconds later, a rope tumbled down the rock like a wet noodle and straightened itself in front of them. Cassie pointed. "You go first. I'll follow."

The two women scaled the rock, gripping the rope and digging their boots into the manmade crevices. Bodhi gripped Elena's wrist and yanked her over the last step, then reached for Cassie.

"I'm coming, Dad. Give me a second." She dabbed her forehead with a handkerchief and fanned her reddened face with her fingers. "Whew."

She heaved a breath, gripped his wrist, and placed her other hand on a loose rock on the face of the mound. A scream echoed. Bodhi nearly lost his grip. He slid down the rock towards Cassie and pulled her by the armpits into his arms, dragging her atop the mound.

She heaved a quivering breath. "Oh, my God, that was close."

"Too close. That'd have been a long drop, Cass. I'm sorry I dragged you along, baby."

"It's okay. Not your fault. I'll suck it up." She grimaced, heaved a breath, and pointed. "Lead the way."

They traveled a mile and a half along a small trail leading to a dead end. A massive vertical rock face blocked them from traveling further.

Bodhi examined the rock, running his hands over a smooth area. "Look. The rock is worn in three distinct places. Maybe these were once the waterfalls right here." He tapped his finger on the map.

"Bodhi, over here … Mira." She pointed. "These white stones don't look like a natural formation. They're intentionally stacked. And the scattered ones don't seem to fit the environment. I'm not a rock expert, but they don't belong here."

Bodhi's eyes lit up. "I think we may have found our spot."

They spent over half an hour rearranging the stones like a Jenga puzzle until they formed a dais with three equal pillars, then plopped in the shade, swigging from their water bottles. Bodhi dabbed his glistening face with his shirt, grunting as he pushed off the ground and rose. Reaching into his backpack, he removed the relics and placed them individually on the three pillars.

Cassie rested her hands on her hips and sighed. "Now what?"

He removed a small journal and leafed through it like a pastor on Sunday, about to give a sermon. "Now I use my best singing voice to fire up the relics … then we'll see what happens."

He hummed, chanted, and repeated the words from the journal.

The air crackled and hissed, filling their nostrils with a pungent scent of an electrical fire. A brilliant emerald beam burst to life, connecting the relics in a perfect triangle.

Before Bodhi could step inside the triangle, thumping whirls whipped up a suffocating red cloud of dust. A steel helicopter emerged like a bird of prey, strafing the ground with gunfire.

"Take cover!" Bodhi shouted.

Elena clutched Cassie's hand and jerked her behind a pillar of rock. Bodhi dove inside the triangle, his heart pounding into his throat.

Agent Abara's voice boomed over a loudspeaker as the craft landed near the site. "Those were warning shots, Doctor McMullin! Stay where you are. We *will* use force if you act foolishly. Drop to your knees and place your hands behind your head. I will not warn you a second time."

Bodhi complied, locking eyes with Cassie peering from her hiding spot. He shook his head the moment his eyes connected with Elena's, begging her to stay hidden.

Agent Abara, Phillip, and two agents dressed in SWAT gear leaped from the chopper onto the flat stone floor. The SWAT agents scooped Bodhi by the armpits and forced him to crouch on a nearby rock, weapons jammed in his ribcage.

Abara grinned—his pearly whites almost glowing. "Ah, Doctor, you have everything laid out with precise detail. My apologies for our abrupt entrance. Have we interrupted something?"

Abara squatted next to Bodhi and rested his hand on his shoulder. "Thank you for using your American Express. It made tracking your movements much easier."

Abara rose, tapped his two agents on the shoulder, and pointed towards Elena and Cassie.

"You can come out now and join the good doctor. Elena? Cassie? No harm will come to you, as long as you cooperate."

They hesitated, then emerged, followed by the agents with gun barrels pressed against their spines. Abara waved a calming hand towards the agents. "That won't be necessary, gentlemen."

Elena spat on Abara's polished combat boots and sneered.

He glanced at his boot and glared at Elena, narrowing his eyes. "Now, that was rude, Elena. Have a seat next to the doctor, please."

Elena and Cassie huddled around Bodhi.

Abara laid his hand on Phillip's shoulder. "Are you ready to make history? Or should I say, 'rewrite history?' Your destiny awaits, my friend." Abara made a sweeping gesture and smiled. "Collect the relics, Phillip, and let us be on our way. Our mission awaits, and there's no time to waste."

"No!" Bodhi shouted. "Phillip, you have no idea what you're doing."

"I have no choice, son. This is the only way I can be with Ethel."

"Time will implode if you attempt to do what you're planning. Phillip … *Dad.* I'm begging you. Don't do this."

Abara pulled a pistol from a holster inside his black leather vest and positioned himself behind Bodhi, Elena, and Cassie.

"Do not interfere, Doctor. We are only here for the relics and will soon be on our way. I'm disappointed you failed to grasp the bigger picture and join us. What we do now is for the greater good of our country and the world."

Bodhi faced Abara. "It's not. I've seen the future. You're meddling with things beyond your understanding. Your actions will doom the planet to complete annihilation. Life will no longer exist. I'm begging you not to do this. Allow me to finish what I started. Think of your wife, your two boys. If you take the relics, you've sealed their fate."

"That seems a bit dark and over the top. I wish you the best, Doctor McMullin, and your family. Once we are gone, you are free to leave. We will not trouble you again."

Phillip marched toward the triangular band of light and paused. He glanced at Bodhi, widening his eyes, his lips forming a half smile. "It's going to be fine, son. I promise, I won't screw this up." He ducked beneath the light band and planted his feet in the center of the triangle, raising his hands to the heavens, closing his eyes, and chanting in an ancient language.

Abara leaned into Bodhi and whispered, "Your father can take it from here."

Bodhi craned his neck toward Abara. "Prepare for eternal damnation. You've unleashed hell on us all."

Sparkling bands of emerald light swirled and intensified with each word from Phillip's lips. Gyrations thrummed like the sixth string of a guitar, amplified a thousand times. Bodhi hugged Elena and Cassie as they covered their ears to muffle the terrifying oscillations.

Vibrant hues erupted, forming a glowing dome of pulsating energy that sealed the triangle. Phillip and the agents looked like lab rats beneath a shimmering glass bowl. Phillip shrieked—pulses of green lightning surged through his body and discharged from his fingertips into the dome, like a magician's plasma ball. He blinked, his eyes widening with panic.

Colors culminated and intensified. A blinding, radiant white light detonated beneath the dome like a silent nuclear blast. The agents vanished. Phillip collapsed. The dome dissipated, releasing the blazing emerald bond that connected the relics.

Bodhi sprang from his seat, blindly reaching for Abara, digging his fingers into the agent's right shoulder. He drove his forehead into the bridge of Abara's nose and tackled him to the ground. The men grappled in the razor-sharp gravel, each struggling for an advantage. Abara shoved his pistol into the base of Bodhi's neck, but Bodhi punched his finger behind the trigger and bit Abara's wrist, fighting to wrestle the pistol free. The weapon fired. Bodhi snatched and flung it, wedging it between a rock and the base of a juniper tree, ten feet away.

Bodhi clamped his right hand around Abara's neck, forcing him onto his back. Abara delivered a bone-crushing knee into Bodhi's ribs and hacked him in the throat with a swift chop. Bodhi wheezed and rolled to his side, gasping. Abara leaped to his feet and kicked Bodhi in the face, knocking him out cold.

As he turned toward the juniper tree to retrieve his pistol, Elena's eyes darkened like a midnight storm. She raised the weapon and shouted, "On the ground, bastardo. Hands behind your head!"

Blood poured from Cassie's chest. Elena screamed, jerking Bodhi's arm and shaking him. "Wake up! Bodhi, wake up! Cassie's been shot!"

He moaned and stretched his jaw, one eye squinting while the other focused on Cassie. "Oh, God! Blondie?"

Cassie lay in a pool of blood, gasping, reaching for Bodhi as the light in her eyes faded.

"I'm here, sweetheart. Hang on … it's going to be okay. Daddy's got you, baby. Cassie? Cassie! God, no!" He rocked her in his arms as her life force drained.

Phillip limped toward them, raising the Mariner's Compass in his right hand and gripping a leather sack with his left.

"Drop the pistol, Elena."

She gripped it with both hands and pointed it towards his face. "Drop the relics, Phillip, or God help you, I'll put a bullet in your skull."

Phillip chanted, suspending Elena before she could pull the trigger, then motioned toward Abara. "Let's go, I have the relics."

Abara nodded towards Bodhi. "My apologies, Doctor. I'm truly sorry for your daughter." Abara waved to the pilot as if twirling a lasso. The blackbird's rotors whirred and roared, stirring up a cloud of red and pelting them with sand.

"Phillip!" Bodhi shouted, tears streaming. "She's my only daughter. She's your only grandchild. For once in your life, do the right thing. I'm begging you."

Phillip paused, glancing at Abara, then at Bodhi. Abara tapped Phillip's shoulder. "We need to go. There's no time."

"Give me two minutes with my son, or our deal is off." Phillip turned and knelt by Cassie. "I'm sorry this happened, son."

Bodhi grasped his wrist. "We can fix this … Help me fix this. Please."

Phillip glanced at the chopper, leaped to his feet, and climbed into the aircraft. Bodhi wailed, hugging Cassie, soaked in her blood. "Cass … hang on, baby. Daddy's got you … I got you…"

The whirring stopped—the chopper suspended five feet above the rock. Phillip leaped to the ground and marched toward them, pointing a stern finger at Bodhi.

"Promise me you'll send me back to Ethel, and I'll help you save Cassie. Promise or I swear I'm out of here, Bodhi."

"I promise. Anything, please help us," he sobbed.

Phillip released Elena and handed Bodhi the timepiece and Tempus Glass. "Alright … We do this together."

Elena slid the pistol into the front of her jeans and snatched the Tempus Glass from Bodhi's hand. They formed a circle around Cassie and sang, matching pitch with the vibrations humming from the relics.

The whirring of rotors resumed. Abara leaped from the chopper and pointed an AK-47 at Phillip. "Get in the chopper, Phillip. Now!"

Elena fired a shot, nicking Abara's right elbow.

Phillip began to chant the moment Abara returned fire. A stray bullet ricocheted, ripping a hole through Phillip's abdomen, knocking him to his knees. Elena fired a single bullet that tore through Abara's right eye, dropping him instantly.

Bodhi stretched his arm toward Phillip, but he pushed him away. "No, let's do this … let's save my granddaughter," he said, holding a bloody hand to his stomach.

A whirlwind swallowed them. They returned to the moment before the scuffle with Abara, repeating the moments before Cassie was shot.

The events repeated—vibrant hues erupted, forming a glowing dome of pulsating energy that draped over the triangle. Phillip and the agents looked like lab rats beneath a shimmering glass bowl. Phillip shrieked—pulses of green lightning surged through his body and discharged from his fingertips into the dome, like a magician's plasma ball.

Colors culminated and intensified. A blinding, radiant white light detonated beneath the dome.

This time, Bodhi did nothing, shielding Cassie and Elena with his body.

Phillip limped toward them, the Mariner's Compass in his right hand, and a leather bag in his left. Abara stood, confused. He raised his fingers to his right eye and glared at Elena as if expecting blood.

As Abara raised the AK-47, he froze. The whirring ceased.

Phillip handed Bodhi the compass and rested his hand on Bodhi's shoulder. "Send me back, Bodhi. Send me back to Ethel. You gave me your word. I saved Cassie, now it's your turn."

"I'm sorry, Phillip, I can't do that. She doesn't love you."

"You gave me your word. Abara had no intention of sending me back. You're my only hope, son. Send me back so I can fix my mistakes. Please. I can't live without her."

"You have to, Phillip. My mother found peace. You need to respect that and find your own peace."

"Then send me back to my wedding day. I'll change. I'll do things different this time. You have my word. I'll make things right…"

"I can't risk that, Phillip. I'm sorry. I won't send you to a time where you can affect the welfare or future of my family."

He hung his head and knelt. "Then where should I go?"

"To the future. To the distant future. Where you can start your life over. A place where nothing has happened yet—where you can choose your path and make your life right without hurting others."

Phillip raised his eyes. "I'm sorry, son, for all the hurt I caused you and your mother."

"You saved my Cassie, Phillip. At that moment, I forgave everything." Bodhi extended his hand. "It's time to go, Dad."

Bodhi handed Elena the Tempus Glass and Cassie the timepiece while he held the Mariner's Compass in his right hand.

Phillip rose, pulled Bodhi toward him, and hugged him, slapping his back. "I guess I'm ready then."

Phillip ripped the compass from Bodhi's hand and shoved him backward. "I'm sorry, Bodhi. I can't live without Ethel. He chanted, aiming the compass toward them.

Elena raised the pistol and blew a hole through Phillip's wrist, dropping him to his knees. "A snake that sheds its skin is still a snake."

Bodhi scooped the compass off the ground and glanced at Cassie and Elena. The group surrounded Phillip as he stretched his arm toward Bodhi and cried, "Wait … listen … we need to …"

In a brilliant flash, Phillip disappeared through a rip in time towards a distant and unknown future. Bodhi directed his attention towards Abara and the pilot. A second portal opened and swallowed them like a vacuum. Bodhi planted himself on a rock and heaved a deep, quivering breath.

"Where'd you send them, Dad?"

"You don't want to know, Blondie."

He smiled at Elena. "How'd you learn to shoot like that, Tex?"

"I told you. I have skills. You don't know everything about me, Bodhi McMullin."

Bodhi restored the relics to the pillars, wrapped his arm around Elena, and took Cassie by the hand.

"I have to finish this."

"No, Dad. Please. Let's just go home."

"There won't be a home, Blondie, if I don't."

"Dad. Why do you have to be the hero every fricking time? Why can't someone else do it?"

"I'm not a hero, Cass. I'm just a man who loves his family."

Elena rested her hand on Cassie's shoulder and kissed Bodhi on the cheek. "You both need to talk." She crossed her arms and stepped away.

"Cass, there's no one else who can do this. It's on me. I'm so sorry, honey. I know it's been hard at times. I do my best ... I try too hard. But it's 'cause I love you so damn much." His eyes glistened.

"Dad? What are you talking about?"

"I know I've failed you at times, Blondie. But my heart was always in the right place. Everything I've accomplished in this life was for you, sweetie ... only you.

"Dad..."

"Let me finish. The day I held you in my arms for the first time, I cried like a baby. Your pink little legs, your face all scrunched up, and that full head of blonde curls. You were so tiny. So helpless. All I wanted to do was keep you safe ... not let anyone hurt you. The doctor called me *Dad*. No one called me that before. It was poetic." He wiped his eyes and wrapped his long arms around her, pulling her in for one of his famous bear hugs.

"Watching you grow up has been the honor of my life, Blondie. Life's greatest gift. Forgive me, Cass, for not always being the best father I could be. Always remember; Your daddy loves you with all his heart and I'm so damn proud of you. You're so much better than me."

She rested her palm on his cheek. "You never let me down, Daddy. You were always there. Always. I wasn't even allowed to fall off my bike without you scooping me up before I could skin my knees. Your biggest flaw was not letting me skin my knees, Dad. You're not perfect, but you're the perfect father for me, and I'm not better than you ... because I'm just like you. There's nothing to forgive. You were my first love, and you taught me to say *no* and stand up for myself. To never settle for anything less than what I deserve. Those lessons are forever written in my heart. I hear your voice in every decision I make. God, how you've burned your lessons into my brain. Whenever I pick up a cereal box, I read the label to see which ingredient is going to kill me next. When I speed down the freeway, I hear your voice yelling inside my head to slow down. I stopped wearing earbuds as a kid because you said they would fry my brain. And the brain-eating amoebas you warned me about. Ugh. I go to the gym because of you … I eat healthy because of you. You're such a pain in the ass, but you know what? I don't know how I could ever live without you, Dad."

"Ah, Cass … everything's going to be alright, sweetheart. I drilled those things into your head on purpose … so you'd always hear my voice."

She sniffled. "And you unintentionally taught me to check the expiration dates on all the food in your fridge. Those dates aren't guidelines, buddy. You need to toss expired food."

He lowered his head and chuckled. "I love you, Blondie. You always make me laugh." He hugged her and kissed her on her forehead. "I need a minute with Elena, sweetheart. Can you give me that?"

"Of course, Daddy. Take your time."

Elena rushed into his arms and crushed his neck with her hug. "Oh, Corazón, I can't let you go. My heart is dying. There must be another way."

"There isn't, my love. I want you to know that my life was made complete the day you found me under that rock, threw me in your wagon, and took me home."

"Qué lástima. You were such a mess. Such a crazy gringo. I never imagined I'd fall so deeply in love with you." She wiped her nose, her sobs mixed with laughter.

"God saved the best for last with you, Elena. The gates of hell couldn't keep us apart. You were always my destiny."

She caressed his cheek and gazed lovingly into his eyes. "And you were mine. Oh, Bodhi, we can hide the relics. Run away from all of this."

"You know that's not true, babe. We have no choice." He shrugged. "The clock's run out. End of the road, I'm afraid."

"Oh, but if only it were me and not you, Mi Amore. I'd take your place—"

"I know you would. Which is why I'm doing this for you and Cassie. So that your lives can go on and have meaning."

She pounded his chest with both fists. "My life has no meaning without you, Corazón," she cried.

He cradled her face. "Our souls are connected, and we'll meet again, my love. I promise."

Cassie wrapped her arms around Bodhi and Elena, sniffling and trembling.

Bodhi heaved a breath and whispered, "Time to go."

"Daddy, no. Dad? No."

Elena and Cassie embraced, tears flooding their cheeks as Bodhi stepped inside the triangle like a lamb to slaughter. He gazed at them and winked, eyebrows arched. Holding his hand to his heart, he mouthed, "I love you," smiling that cantankerous juvenile smile, they adored, reflecting the boy inside the man.

Bodhi closed his eyes and raised his hands to the heavens. He muttered prayers and chants as sparkling emerald bands of light energized around him. A flash of white light exploded, transporting him into oblivion.

TWENTY-TWO

A radiant presence emerged before Bodhi, towering like an ancient oak, yet weightless as light itself. Its form shimmered with the brilliance of a living nebula, tendrils of celestial color rippling outward in waves that defied comprehension. Around the being, an aura pulsed, deeper and more vibrant than any earthly rainbow, each hue humming with silent power. Its eyes blazed like molten suns, and when it spoke, its voice was thunderous, infinite, and eternal. At its feet, the three relics hovered in reverent orbit, slowly ascending into the air like planets drawn into divine gravity, each one igniting with an inner radiance as they came to rest above the being's outstretched hands. Bodhi's breath caught inside his chest. He knew without doubt, without question, this was Cassiel. He dropped to his knees, trembling before the unimaginable majesty of the angel.

"You have served well, Son of Humanity. You are discharged from your travels." The angel raised his hand over Bodhi and disappeared with the relics, now in their celestial form.

Bodhi plummeted like a rock into smothering darkness, plunging into an ocean of glittering jeweled lights, his body washed upon a vast beach of golden sands. Filling his lungs with warm, briny air, he rose and reluctantly opened his eyes. A sunset lit the ocean on fire like loving strokes from a Van Gogh brush. The beach was familiar—Stinson Beach, California—but somehow perfect. Too perfect.

His toes pressed into the warm sand as he strolled through the salty breezes and spotted a lone house in the distance. Gram's beach house—but where are all the neighbors? There wasn't so much as a gum wrapper on the beach. Everything was pristine. The wood in Gram's home no longer bleached and weathered.

When he reached the porch, a stunning young woman in a golden summer dress with long, fiery orange locks relaxed on the porch swing, one leg beneath the other, arms crossed, and a smirk across her strawberry lips. Sparkling sapphire eyes pierced his soul.

Bodhi asked, "Excuse me … is this heaven? Are you an angel?"

"I've been called many things in my life, but only one man ever called me *Angel*. And it wasn't you, dear boy."

"I don't understand … why am I here?"

"This is your purgatory. A place where you must resolve all of your fears, all of your guilt, and all of your pain. It's a layover to your final destination. We must heal your brokenness if you are to move on with your life."

"What life? I'm dead, aren't I?"

"There is no death. You are as much alive now as you've always been. Even more so."

"But you called this my purgatory. I'm in Hell, then?"

"No, James. You're not in Hell, sweet boy. You're in transition."

"Wait … Gram? Is that you in there?"

"Who else would it be, James? This is *my* house, silly boy."

"Oh, my God … you're … you're so beautiful."

"Goodness, Lord. Between you and Cassie, you'd think I was never young. Yes, James. Aren't I a peach? A real babe. No wonder your grandfather couldn't keep his hands to himself." She giggled.

"So, what now? What do I do, Grammy? My heart is broken … I can't breathe. I've lost Elena. Lost Cassie. Am I to wander this version of Stinson Beach forever?"

Gram patted the seat next to her. "Come. Sit next to me, James."

Bodhi surrendered to the soft cushions and Gram's warm hug around his waist. The flood gates opened. He buried his face in his hands and sobbed.

"That's good. Let it all out, my precious boy. A good cry cleanses the soul and reconnects you with your true self like fresh air after rain."

"I'm so lost, Gram. Is Cassie going to be okay? How will Elena go on without me?"

"They're going to be fine, James. First, let's look at your life, my boy. All the things you've done, good and bad. How you made others feel, how the decisions you made and the ones you neglected affected the lives of others. All the patients you healed and the lives you saved. Gaze into the sunset with me."

A panoramic view of Bodhi's life played out before him like a million movie clips at warp speed. Reliving each moment, understanding fully the impact of his words and actions, and how they played out over time.

"You made the ultimate sacrifice. You gave up your life to save Cassie and Elena's. To save your grandchildren, the human race, and every creature upon the Earth."

"Grandchildren?"

"Oh, yes. Cassie had another child. Would you like to see them?"

She pointed at the sky. "That's young William."

"Does he become a quarterback?"

"The best quarterback in *USC* history."

"USC? No, no, no…"

"I'm teasing. He never liked sports, James. He grew tall and handsome and followed in your footsteps to become a respected neurosurgeon. It's the other one that inherited your athleticism."

"Is he a quarterback?"

"*She* ... James. Your granddaughter, Jamie Elena Cooper."

A lump the size of a melon filled his throat as he fought back more tears. "Jamie Elena?"

"Now that one has a rocket of an arm. First-team All-American pitcher for the UCLA Bruins softball team. Her major is Economics, and her minor is in History. Sharp as a tack, that one ... feisty like her grandmother. Must be the red hair she inherited." Gram flipped her hair and grinned.

"I missed everything, Gram. They'll never know me."

"They know everything about you, dear boy."

"What about Elena?"

"I'm afraid she's broken, James. Losing you and Cassie shattered her heart into a thousand pieces."

"Me *and* Cassie? What do you mean? They were together when I left."

"When you completed the ritual, they were sent back in time. Cassie to the nineteen forties with William and their children, and Elena to eighteen-sixty-six. It was a consequence of the reset."

"What happens to me, Gram? You haven't answered my question."

"That is a decision *you* will need to make, James. When you've learned to forgive yourself and understand who you truly are and where you belong in the scheme of history, you'll be ready."

"Ready for what?"

"Ready to move on. Ready to choose."

"Choose what? This is all too confusing. I feel helpless to fix it."

"Your selflessness moved the Creator of all things. You touched His heart, and He granted you another chance at life, dear. But ... You can only choose *one* life. A life as a father and grandfather with Cassie, or a life as a husband with Elena."

"What? That's not a choice. I can't give one of them up? That's wrong … it isn't fair. You can't ask me to do that. Why?"

"Because they live in different times. And you can no longer traverse time, my dear boy."

"How do I choose? I don't think I can."

"You can visit them in their dreams, James. Meditate, and when they sleep, you can bring them here. That's how you'll decide."

Bodhi leaned on the porch rail, staring at the blazing sunset that hadn't moved since he arrived, remaining inches above the water. He smacked a wooden beam and turned toward Gram.

"But how … Gram? Gram?"

The empty porch swing squeaked as it swayed in the gentle breeze.

"Don't leave me here alone. Please."

Bodhi wandered down the steps and sauntered across the wet sand toward the water's edge, foam rushing past his ankles. He closed his eyes and pictured Cassie as a child. His heart fluttered from an abysmal ache. Lifting his eyes to the heavens, he followed the path of a single gull as it soared over the ocean, then vanished. Tears streamed down his cheeks, his chest tightened, stealing his breath.

A gentle hand slid into his. "Daddy? What are you doing out here?"

He whipped his body around, stunned at her presence. It was Cassie. But a seventeen-year-old Cassie. He gathered her in his arms and sobbed.

"Blondie? Are you really here with me?"

"Of course, I am. Who else calls you Daddy?" She frowned and raised a brow. "Uh … don't answer that. I, uh, really don't think I want to know," she tittered.

He cradled her face and directed her eyes towards his. "You're dreaming, aren't you, Cass?"

191

"Yes, Dad. But hey, it's a beautiful dream. I've missed you so, so much."

"Cass, we have to talk."

"I know. Gram told me."

"She did? Okay, well ... Gram wants me to make an impossible choice. Either a life where I'm a grandpa with you, or one where I'm a husband to Elena."

He fell to his knees. "I can't choose, Cass. I can't. I love you both so much. My heart is ripping apart." He wrapped his arms around her waist.

Cassie kneeled and hugged his neck, resting her head on his shoulder.

"Daddy, I have my life with William. I have the kids. You have a granddaughter, by the way."

He chuckled. "Grams showed me. I love her name, Blondie."

"The point is, I don't want you to be alone. I don't want you living your life for me. You gave me everything I ever needed, so it's okay to let go now. It's okay to be happy, and as much as I know how bad I'll miss you, I want you to live out your life with Elena. I could never bear to watch you suffer, knowing how empty your life would be without her."

She wiped the tears from his cheeks. "I can ride a bike by myself now, Dad. I can walk to school alone. You don't have to cook for me or clean up after me. You don't have to dry my eyes when a boy breaks my heart. I have William, and he'll never break my heart. Go. Enjoy your happiness. Find Elena and live out your life. You need her ... she needs you. And I need to know that you have each other. Please. Do that for me, Daddy."

"Ah, Cass. I love you so much, sweetheart. I just ... can't let go."

"I know you love me, Dad. It's alright. You can do it. Let go now."

She walked backwards and faded into the soft amber light. "I have to go now. I love you, Daddy."

"Cass? Cassie?" he mumbled, collapsing on the beach, grabbing handfuls of wet sand and gazing into the sunset. "Sweet dreams, Blondie."

≈

Bodhi strolled along the beach and climbed the steps to Gram's beach house, plopping onto the porch swing. He reflected on his life, Cassie and Elena, his medical practice, and Cassie's mother, Savanna. There are so many things he could have done better. Mistakes he wished he hadn't made. The worst was losing Cassie in the park when she was six. That episode will forever haunt him. He slid down the seat, folded his arms, and closed his eyes.

"Have you spoken to Elena, James?"

He jerked and sat upright. "Oh, jeez, Gram. You scared the crap out of me. No, not yet. I-I'm not ready."

"Why aren't you ready? What's the holdup?"

"Gram, I'm kind of struggling here, okay? I'm still trying to wrap my head around the choices you gave me."

"Do you like it here, James?"

"It's beautiful. I always loved your beach house. But as beautiful as it is, it isn't the same place, and it's always sunset. So, no. I guess I don't."

She smacked his shoulder. "Then snap out of it and decide, or you'll be spending a lot of time here *reflecting* on your life instead of *living* it."

"It's not that easy, Gram. I don't want to make the wrong decision."

"There is no wrong decision, James. Search your heart. Face your fears. Let go of all the pain and look at your life objectively. Only then can you know the path, dear. Your hesitation is what's keeping you here. And it's keeping me from seeing Thomas and Joseph."

He crinkled his brow. "You're seeing both of them? That's a bit messed up, Gram … even for you."

She swatted his arm. "That's none of your business. Your job is to get up off your behind, dust yourself off, and make a darn decision."

"I love Elena with all my heart, Gram. More than life. I can't live without her. But I'd die for Cassie, and I need to protect her and keep her safe. I didn't always protect her, Grammy." Emotion constricted the base of his throat, making it hard to breathe.

She slid her hand into his. "You always protected her, James—overprotected her. You barely let her breathe. Let go of your fear. All parents make mistakes and fail sometimes. It's how we learn to be parents. Our children are the ones who teach us those valuable lessons."

"But I lost her in the park overnight, Gram. I'll never forgive myself for that. The terror she must have felt and the bad things that could have happened eat at my soul. It haunts me, still."

"Let me show you something you never knew, darling. Look at the sunset."

An image of little Cassie holding a woman's hand reflected in the clouds as they strolled along a familiar sidewalk.

"What is this, Gram?"

"It's Cassie. And that is her mom, walking her home. You spent the entire evening looking for her, and when you arrived home, you fell asleep in her room. Cassie was safe all along—in bed with her mother behind a locked door. Fast asleep. Savanna wanted to teach you a harsh lesson. And a ruthless lesson it turned out to be."

"I don't understand."

"Savanna walked to the park to meet you and Cassie. She found Cassie alone at the other end of the playground, and when she saw you distracted by your cell phone, it triggered her, so she took Cassie home to punish you by making you think you lost her. She was never lost, dear boy."

He sat with his jaw agape. Speechless. Dumbfounded.

"That's so … All this time, I thought she wandered the streets alone, in the dark. I pictured her crying … calling out for me."

"No, James. That's not what happened. You're a wonderful father. Whatever crazy notion Savanna had of teaching you such a mean-spirited lesson only traumatized you all these years. But as wrong as that was, you need to forgive her."

His face flushed, and his neck prickled. "I can't…"

"You were both young parents, and she was very jealous of you at the time. And angry that your medical practice kept you away from her. Forgive her, James."

"How can I, Grams? How do I forgive *that*?"

"The same way I forgave you when you nailed my favorite pair of shoes to the porch. I nearly fell and broke my neck. I cussed you like a preacher stuck in traffic. Then I had the best laugh I've had in years."

"Oh, man, I forgot about that. I'm so sorry." He guffawed.

"No, you're not. Close your eyes, dear. Elena has fallen asleep and is waiting to see you. Go to her, James."

He closed his eyes and heaved a breath as gentle hands slid inside his and tugged at him. The milky scent of her skin filled his nostrils. His eyes opened to her stateliness and eloquent charm. The tailored fit of her black riding habit and high-leather boots accentuated her voluptuous figure and radiant olive skin. Her long raven hair flowed in waves that cascaded over her shoulders like satin. The flecks of coffee in her large emerald eyes seduced him and set his heart on fire, stealing his breath.

This was the Elena who commanded respect. The Union spy whose valor exceeded the bravest soldier and whose courageous deeds were etched into American history. He sat in awe of her, unable to speak.

"Ride with me, Mi Amore," she commanded.

They rode two beautiful white stallions along the beach, the tide washing over their hoofs. "I've missed you, Corazón? Why do you allow yourself to suffer so?"

"I can't choose my path, my love, and it's breaking my heart."

"I cannot tell you what to do, Mi Amore. But I can tell you this: I will wait for you until I've breathed my last breath. I love you too much to ask you to follow me. You must follow your own heart. You are my eternal love, and you hold my very soul in your hands. I love you always, Bodhi." Elena yanked her reins, turned, and trotted into the ocean.

"Wait. Elena, wait!" He raced after her, but she faded into the glittery waves. Emptiness washed over him like an abandoned gravestone.

Bodhi wandered back to the beach house and sat alone on the porch swing, going through the pages of his life like a photo album. His anger at Savanna's betrayal filled him with grief. How could someone he loved since childhood want to hurt him so deeply? Did he neglect his marriage, pushing Savanna into an irrational state? How deeply he must have hurt her. But it doesn't excuse what she did. It was unjust and cruel.

The knowledge that Cassie was never alone and scared, never crying out for him to rescue her that night, comforted him now. The years of unbearable guilt weighing on him and his fear faded in self-reflection and a profound understanding.

He whispered, "I forgive you, Savi. I'm sorry I hurt you by putting myself and my career first. I shouldn't have done that. We were kids. We made so many mistakes … *I* made so many mistakes."

A tender hand caressed his. "And you learned from those mistakes, dear."

"Ah, Gram. Stop sneaking up on me like that."

She giggled. "Why? The look on your face is priceless."

"Why do we do the things we do, Gram? Things that serve ourselves and hurt the ones we love? Why?"

196

"Because we're human, James. Stop being so hard on yourself. Savanna wasn't innocent in all of this. You both contributed equally."

"But what about Cass? I let her down too many times. I wouldn't allow her to walk to school without following her. I couldn't let her out of my sight."

"It's the price of being a parent and an over-protective father who worships his only daughter. James, let me tell you something. The abandonment you suffered as a boy is the trigger that drove your protectiveness for Cassie. It was driven by fear and insecurities of an abusive childhood, and caused you to cling to Cassie. To want to keep her safe every second of every day. The greatest gift you can give your child is their independence, my dear. You must teach someone you can't live without, how to live without you. A mother bird pushes her young from the nest. It breaks her heart in doing so, but her love forces her to teach them to survive without her. You've given Cassie all the tools she needs. You taught her well, my boy. She'll be alright, and she can make her own decisions … and her own mistakes. Listen to her advice for once in your life, James."

He rose and kissed Gram on the cheek, then ambled along the edge of the seashore, skipping shells across the water, causing shimmering reflections to burst into thousands of tiny sparkles. For the first time, his heart was at peace, and his mind seemed clear.

As Bodhi strolled back toward the beach house, the sun dipped below the water for the first time. A dense fog blew in from the ocean and swallowed him. When the fog lifted, lush, grassy fields surrounded him. He strolled past a farmhouse, toward a small hill, and paused. Atop the hill, faint whimpers carried in the wind. He slogged up the bank and spied a figure kneeling between two graves with a pistol in her trembling hand pressed to her temple.

"Elena?"

She turned, her reddened eyes moist and swollen. Tossing the pistol, she leaped from the ground and rushed into his arms, screaming, "Bodhi! Oh, Bodhi! ¡Es un milagro! Am I dreaming? Did I die? Oh, Mi Corazón! How did you find me? How is that possible?"

"No, my love. You're not dreaming, and you didn't die. I'm here. I don't know how, but I'm here."

She wrapped her arms around his neck and her legs around his torso, bursting into uncontrollable sobs.

"Mi Amore … Mi Amore, how can this be? How can you be here with me?"

Bodhi swung her into his arms and carried her down the hill into the farmhouse. He laid her on the bed and gently kissed her lips.

"Not here, Corazón," she whispered. "We must leave this place."

"Where should we go?" he asked.

"To your home in California. Stinson Beach."

"According to the history books I've read, there's not much there, and it's a bit of a challenge to get to. We'll need horses, supplies…"

"Then we'll be among the first, and I'll teach you to be a better rider. Where's your sense of adventure, husband?"

Bodhi crossed his arms. "I'm up to the challenge, but I don't think my credit card will buy us a pair of horses. What do we do for money?"

Elena removed several tin cans from beneath a hidden floorboard in her kitchen. She snagged wads of bills from and emptied jars of coins.

"Will this do?"

"Wow. A sugar mama of my very own. The California coast it is. Maybe I'll learn to pan for gold."

She rushed into his arms and hugged his neck. "Hold me, Corazón, and never, never let me go. Promise me we'll die in each other's arms and I can kiss you with my last breath."

"I'll keep that promise, but let's kick that can waaaay down the road for now, huh?"

TWENTY-THREE

Bodhi left a journal of his life with Elena to be mailed to Cassie and William's home in Honolulu after 1950. The journal left instructions on where to locate their joint grave on their farm near Stinson Beach, California.

Cassie visited their gravesite each year on her father's birthday and read a single chapter of the journal out loud each visit. She sat on the white marble bench she and William had dedicated to them years ago, preparing to read the final chapter.

"Oh, Daddy. Happy birthday," she whispered. "I've missed you so much. Your journal is the only thing that's helped me through these many years. William passed last Christmas. He almost made it to ninety. Little William moved to Southern California with his wife. They have three children and lots of grandkids. You'll be thrilled to know that one of them was a quarterback at UCLA. He looks just like you, Dad. And acts like you, too. It's uncanny. I found your smile again in his. And your bear hugs. Oh, those bear hugs. He's always been my favorite. Everyone knew it. It was almost like you returned to me.

"Jamie is divorced. She lives with her daughter in Seattle and has started dating again. I know if you were here, you'd know what to tell her. You always had the answers, even when we didn't want to hear them."

Cassie dabbed her nose with a tissue; her aged hands trembled.

"I don't know if I've ever shared this with you, but Mom died years ago. I didn't want to tell you. Soon after you left us, the cancer came back. You were right. You were always right, Dad. It's funny. The other day, I found myself thinking about 'Stupid Movie Night'. I laughed so hard I almost peed … Then I cried myself to sleep."

She placed a German chocolate cupcake on his gravestone and smiled.

"I made this for you. Your favorite. I've had a good life, Dad. I can't complain. This is the last time I'm going to visit. No more cupcakes. Maybe in a few years, I can crawl into your lap and feel one of your famous bear hugs. Thank you for visiting me in my dreams. You always look so young and handsome … and I always ask, 'Where have you been, Daddy?' But you never answer me. You simply smile that smile I miss so much, and fade into the light. You always look so happy when you go. Well, here goes. The final chapter of your journal, Daddy."

Dear Blondie,

I made a promise to Elena years ago that we would die in each other's arms. I'll have to break that promise now, sweetheart, as Elena isn't cooperating. She's taken such good care of herself that I think she'll live to be a hundred and ten. I'm not going to make it that long, Blondie. They tell me I have a week. Two at best. But what do doctors know, anyway? Right?

You'll notice the handwriting isn't mine. It's Elena's. She's agreed to be my secretary and pen what I tell her. (I didn't agree, Mija, he forced me. He's so bossy.)

She's been so good to me, Cass. I don't know what I would have done without her. People grow old together and become the same person. They lose half of themselves when one of them has to say goodbye. I don't know how the other half can survive. I'm not good with goodbyes. Never was.

As I reflect on my life, I realize so much. How much time I've wasted. How much energy I've spent on foolish pursuits and silly problems. You've taught me so much, Cass.

So much about life and love. I'm a better man for being your father. You might think that God sent me to you, to be your daddy and protect you and teach you all about life, but in truth, God sent you to me, to teach me all those things and more. You are my angel, sweetheart, and loving you has been the greatest privilege of my life.

You sacrificed so much for me, and I've missed you dearly all these years. I'll drop in on you from time to time, Cass. Just know how much your daddy loved and adored you. There are no words to express just how much.

I have to go now, Blondie. Elena has crawled into bed with me so that I can fall asleep in her arms one last time. God bless and keep you, my precious daughter.

Cassie lifted two roses from her bag and laid them on their grave. One red and one white. She used an old paintbrush to clear the dirt and grime from their engraving. "There you go, guys. Good as new," she whispered.

Dr. James Bodhi McMullin
Loving husband, father, grandfather, and time traveler
Star quarterback for the UCLA Bruins
Once saved the world
Born April 3, 1981 Died January 28, 1915

Elena Maria Fernandez Lozano McMullin
Loving wife, mother, nana, and time traveler
A brave and true American heroine
Born February 13, 1837 Died February 25, 1925

Elena slipped away from her body and leaped into a dazzling, spiraling vortex ten years after Bodhi and joined her beloved in eternity, where they walk barefoot and hand-in-hand along Stinson Beach, California. Not a day goes by that she doesn't hold her precious sons, Gabriel and Santiago, in her arms.

Bodhi, Elena, and Will meet every day on Gram's porch, chatting and leaving an empty seat for Cassie. On this particular evening, a young woman with flowing blonde locks raced along the seashore, waving her arms and screaming in the distance.

"William! ... Daddy!"

Dear reader,

"The Timepiece Origin" will be book five and the final book of the Timepiece Series. Book five will tell the original story of Gram—a prequel, in essence. It will answer all the questions about Gram's early life and how this incredible adventure began.

I sincerely hope you have enjoyed the series and encourage you to share it with family and friends who enjoy a good story filled with fantastic travels, romance, family relationships, adventure, and page-turning suspense. It has been my honor to take you on this journey through time.

Thank you for being a loyal reader. Please check out more of my books on my website, AuthorKevinMiller.com. And if you would be so kind, please leave a positive book review on Amazon and Goodreads.

Sincerely,

Kevin

About the Author

An unexpected phone call delivered shocking news to Kevin and his family. His grandfather changed the family name. Instead of the All-American, 'Miller', his real name was the very Polish 'Puchalski'. His grandfather took this secret to his grave to protect an even darker family secret, and it remained hidden for almost a century.

Kevin's first novel, *Heart of Steel: Based on a True Story*, is the story of his grandfather and the secrets and shocking events of his family history. A story so incredible that a Hollywood production company optioned the book for film and television.

Kevin has appeared on television, national talk radio, and podcasts discussing his story and his books.

Kevin served his country in the United States Air Force, receiving college degrees in Electronics Technology and Electronics Engineering. He later changed careers, earning a third degree in Information Technology and Web Management, and spent fourteen years in a major city in Arizona as their Web Developer, where he retired early.

Kevin was born in Canton, Ohio, and grew up in Tempe, Arizona. He and his wife, Annette, have raised two daughters together in the heart of Southern California, where the girls have pursued careers in acting. After a decade spent in sunny California, they moved home to Arizona in 2023. Visit him at AuthorKevinMiller.com.